T0128524

THE BAD BOY
GETS PUNISHED, TWO

A sissy maid missy bad boy series, part five

m missy

authorHOUSE®

AuthorHouse™
1663 Liberty Drive
Bloomington, IN 47403
www.authorhouse.com
Phone: 1-800-839-8640

Published by AuthorHouse   05/09/12.

ISBN: 978-1-4685-8784-5 (sc)
ISBN: 978-1-4685-8783-8 (e)

Contents

LOOKING BACK TO:

The Bad Boy Gets Punished, four

Cally and I went on that cruse that Cally bought for us,

The best and worst weekend of my life,

My life feel apart as

I got arrested,

The Plea Bargain,

My sentencing hearing,

My new life in the place where I am sent to be punished, the Reform Farm,

My continuing relationship with Cally, much to my surprise, but then Cally was always surprising me, as well as, those around us,

It included some unusual punishments in that unusual place,

It included the transformation of me, a young rich, BOSS OF THE HOUSE, to a small submissive obedient boy to others,

It included my transformation from the, Boss of the house, to the submissive obedient young "girlfriend" to Cally,

The Bad Boy Gets Punished, Two

A sissy maid missy bad boy series, part five

Cally and I helped an innocent boy go free,

Cally becomes a financial genius,

I tell Cally of my severe beating from the Boss that left big thick welts from the Boss's strap from my neck to my knees from a strapping that lasted 30 minutes. The punishment was so severe, it took three weeks for the welts and bruises to go away,

I was also whipped for my three month anniversary at the Reform Farm in front of the girls and movie cameras,

The Boss questioned my good deed for LeMond,

The Two white guys, Rick's revenge,

My new clothes,

Cally continues to take over my life and now my punishments,

Humiliating spanking in the barn if front of all the guys, Cally spanks Ally for the first time, Cally's thanksgiving surprise, THE BEST AND WORSE DAY OF MY LIFE!!!!!!!!!!!!!!!!!!!!!!!!!!!!!!

More new clothes,

Cally whips me for the first time,

Chess game and 2 canings,

Cally made me more money, I am becoming Cally's "GOOD GIRL".

INTRODUCTION:

Hello, my name is Morton and this is my story.

I grew up in southwestern Florida just outside of Naples. My twin sister, Mindy, and I were the only children of wealthy parents. We lived in a big house on approximately 10 acres of woods. The house was about 8000 square feet and had a nice pool with waterfalls, a hot tub, and even a diving board.

At 18 years of age I had the most perfect life I could ever imagine. I was the best tennis player in my high school and maybe in the county. My parents sent me to tennis camp every summer and I had lessons throughout the year as well.

I was a great baseball player, especially an outfielder that Willy Mays would be proud. I lead the team with on base percentage and led the league in walks every year.

My twin sister, Mindy, had the same opportunities that I had and was also an excellent tennis player, she did not play baseball.

We seemed to have all the money in the world as my father apparently made a great living and was very rich. So we never had any concerns that many of the other kids our age had.

Both Mindy and me got new cars for our 18th birthday and I should tell you that I became a point of jealousy from the other kids as I drove a $90,000.00 Jaguar. My sister chose a mustang and the other kids seemed to be ok with that choice.

We both got excellent grades in school without much effort and were both considered to be some of the smartest kids in the school. I was sort of the king of the school as I was very popular and most everyone would follow me with any of my opinions.

Discipline was never a real problem as neither my sister or I ever got into any trouble. We did not even have to help clean the house as our parents had a live in maid.

However, my father graduated near the top of his class at West Point and became an army officer, before he became a business man. So, he had little patience for bad behavior.

He taught my sister and me at an early age that you follow the rules or you get punished, Period. My dad use to tell me that was the way of the world and I may as well learn it when I was young enough to adjust to expectations.

My dad made the rules very clear in advance so there was never any surprises. My Father taught us his ten commandments of life, as my father called them.

> One, always be obedient to those you need to obey.

> Two, Always be polite, to everyone, all the time, no matter what.

Three, Always be friendly and nice to everyone, all the time.

Four, Always do the right thing, even when it's hard.

Five, Always be generous.

Six, There is no good reason to drink.

Seven, There is no good reason to smoke.

Eight, There is no good reason to take drugs.

Nine, There is not good reason to gamble.

Ten, always be honest with yourself and others.

Mindy and I learned and followed my Father's 10 commandments of life, most of the time, and were both very happy kids. Every time we were punished, it was because we forgot one of those rules.

From the time we were around 6 years old, if we were naughty, my dad would spank us with his hand on our bare bottoms over his knees and make us stand in the corner. After we turned 10, we would get our spankings, which were very rare, with a hardwood hairbrush. That was never something to look forward to.

Overall, over my 10 years of corporal punishment, from being six years old to 10 years old, I was probably spanked 6 times with my dad's hand. That's only 6 times in 4 years, so I was pretty good. My sister was probably spanked only 3 or 4 times.

From age 10 to 13 for me, I was spanked with the hairbrush only twice, that was twice too many for me. My sister, maybe three times.

From age 13 to 17 I did not enjoy my father's spanking brush about 5 times. I did seem to have a little problem as I went thru puberty and got three spankings that one year. Only one before and one after that 14th year. My sister I think only got one more hairbrush spanking when she was 14 and that was it for her.

A spanking from our father was a sure and very unhappy event. Our father believed in two things when it came to a spanking. One, it should hurt more than enough for you ever to think that disobedience is worth the risk again. Two, it should be as embarrassing as possible, as that was sometimes worse than the spanking itself.

Therefore, a spanking in our house was always a public affair. In other words Mindy or me would be spanked in the living room and whichever child was not being spanked was there to watch the one who was getting the spanking.

Additionally, my mother was there, but the worst part was that the maid, Sabrina, was there also. As Sabrina hated me, she never missed a good smile as she watched me get a spanking. I also noticed that when it was my sister turn to get spanked that Sabrina was not around.

As I said, our father made the spankings as embarrassing as possible. First he made us stand in the corner for about 30 minutes before each spanking, sort of advertizing to everyone else that a spanking was on its way.

Then right there in front of everyone, our father would call us to his side, as he sat on the spanking chair, and lower my pants and underwear. In my sister case, it most likely was lowering her panties and flipping her skirt up over her back, but you get the idea.

The end result was that you had your naked butt out there for everyone to see. In my case everyone got to see my penis also which was almost the most embarrassing part.

That part got worse in my later years as I would also get an erection. So for the last 4 or 5 spankings of my life from my father I had to stand there in front of everyone, especially Sabrina, with an erection.

Now, I had no idea at this point in my life what the erection was all about as I could not see where they were any good for anything, but for some reason, I felt embarrassed that I had one.

For some reason also, for the last two spankings that my sister Mindy got, I also got an erection watching her get her ass bared and especially as it was spanked over my dad's lap and Mindy wiggled it all over the place and my dad spanked her so hard and for so long.

I loved looking at her bare butt and even got a look at her pussy lips. Not that I knew what I was really looking at, she was just different from me. But, for some reason I liked to look.

I loved watching Mindy's ass turn all red, then dark red, then sort of purple, and then some black and blue.

Before my father stopped spanking Mindy my penis was throbbing for some unknown reason to me.

I think the part I liked the best was the crying. I really like to hear Mindy cry as the spanking went on and on and on. I liked it the best when Mindy cried so hard that I knew she had lost complete control of herself as the spanking was hurting her so much.

When I was the one getting the spanking, as I said, I was really embarrassed to have my ass bared in front of Mindy and Sabrina, not so much for my mother. In my later spankings, as I stood in the corner waiting for my spanking, I was worried about having an erection in front of Sabrina. I seemed to get an erection just from thinking about how embarrassed I would get later.

But, the worst part was when I started to cry, just like Mindy cried. I was so embarrassed to cry in front of Mindy, but especially in front of Sabrina. Nevertheless, no matter how hard I wanted not to cry, I could not stop myself as my dad spanked me so hard and for such a long time that I could do nothing but lay there over his lap and take my spanking and cry my eyes out.

Our dad believed that a spanking should be long enough and hard enough so that we remembered it for a long time. But, more importantly, he believed that the spanking should hurt so much and that you should be embarrassed so much that you would not take any more chances on ever getting another one.

Our father always met his goal as neither Mindy nor me ever would take a chance at doing anything that would result in getting a spanking. So, we only got a few, a few too many. But, they were rare and only for doing stupid things that for one reason of another we did not seem to stay out of as after all, we were young stupid kids in a way and made stupid mistakes.

After the spanking was over, we were sent back to the corner for another 30 minutes but we had to stand in the corner without any pants or underwear so everyone one could see our well spanked asses. Both Mindy and I still cried for a while from both the pain of the spanking and the embarrassment of having to stand in the corner showing off our spanked asses.

When it was Mindy's turn to stand in the corner, she had to hold up the back of her skirt to show off her spanked ass. I loved sitting in the living room after Mindy got spanked and just looked at her nice plump ass.

As I got older I did realize that my embarrassment did not actually come all that much from the process of the spanking, the baring of my ass, the erection for all to see, or the crying, but rather, I thought the most embarrassing part was that I was there to be spanked for being bad.

I always felt like a bad kid during those times and the embarrassment I felt from feeling like a bad kid was the part that bothered me the most.

Having told you all this, I do not want you to think that Mindy or me felt like our dad was cruel or mean in anyway. He spent most of his time playing with us, teaching us, and loving us.

Looking back on the growing years, we did not ever

smoke, drink, sniff glue, take drugs, or do any of the other stupid things that many of our friends were doing. So, my dad's theory about spanking seemed to ring true and he kept us out of trouble by making us fear spankings.

THE STORY BEGINS:

However, this story, my story to you, started when Mindy and I were 18 years old and our parents were killed when their own private plane crashed in Alaska when they were on vacation and got stuck in a sudden snow storm.

They left all of their assets to my sister and I in a trust fund which amounted to over 10 million dollars. My sister and I would get equal shares of the income from the trust until we were 25 years old and then we would be given our shares of the trust outright. The income amounted to about over 30,000.00 per month for each of us, after taxes.

Now, considering we lived in a fully paid 2 million dollar house we certainly did not need all that money to pay the household bills, so the trustee paid all our bills, gave us each an allowance, and allowed the trust amount to keep on growing.

However, as Mindy and I were just 18 years old, the trust required that we have an adult guardian live with us until we were 21 years old.

My Mother's request within the trust asked us to take in her best friend, Molly, as our guardian, together with her twin daughters, Ally and Cally.

My sister and I agreed to honor our dead Mother's

wishes and have Molly and her twin daughters come live in our house with Molly as our guardian. Molly really needed this break as she did not make very much money and her husband, who left her five years earlier, was not paying any child support.

As both my sister and I knew Molly and her two girls very well, it seemed to be a good fit for everyone as both my sister and I liked the three of them. Our only obligation under the trust fund was to have at least one guardian live with us as Mindy and I were under 21 at the time. So, this solution seemed to be an easy answer.

My name is Morton, Mort for short and as I said I was 18 years old. Although I was a very good tennis player and baseball player, I was only five foot seven inches tall but was hoping to get taller in my later teenage years.

However, that may only be a hope and a prayer as my mom was only five foot tall and my dad was only five foot eight inches tall. No one in my mother's or father's family was much taller, so most likely I would end up being just be too short for my own liking.

In addition to being short, I was also small. I only weighed about 125 pounds and had a 28 inch waist line. The only place I seemed to have any muscles was in my ass and thighs. For some reason I had developed a nice size and nicely shaped ass and two large thighs.

However, my sister would tell me that I had such nice looking legs for a guy. Mindy called them "girly" legs. Some of her girl friends use to tease me about my "girly" legs as well, but it was all in fun, more fun for them than me, but it was alright.

I worked out a lot over the past few years hoping to build some muscles to make up for my small size and that seemed to help but it mostly just seemed to help maintain my thighs and nice ass. The bottom line here was that I was too small to ever really considering playing profession sports.

However, I also seemed to be a good looking young fellow as I did not seem to have any problem attracting the attention of the girls. In fact, I was able to date almost any girl I wanted.

Apparently I was pretty smart also as I got almost straight "A"s in a Catholic school without much effort. Usually, I did not even have to study or do much homework, I heard the teacher explain something once and I just knew it.

I guess to be fair as I am going to tell you about the bodies of the females in this house, I should note the in addition to being short and skinny I also had a short penis. The poor thing was only about five inches long but it was pretty fat, not that that helps much, so I guess I will be no stud in the dating life as I get older. Maybe it will still grow some, but as with my height, that is just a hope and a prayer.

MINDY:

My Sister's name is Mindy, (yes, we are Mort and Mindy). Mindy was also very short, only five foot two inches tall, but she did have a nice set of full round tits and a nice plump ass. Mindy had long brown hair, a great smile, and was very nice looking. Mindy was also real smart and got good marks in school without much effort.

As with me and girls, Mindy did not seem to have any problems getting the attention of any male creatures and seemed to have her pick of any guy she wanted.

My Sister and I were real good friends and could discuss anything, even our sexual lives as they developed.

MOLLY:

My mother's best friend was Molly and she was about 38 years old and was five foot nine inches tall. Molly had medium length brown hair, small tits, nice sexy legs, and she had a nice full round ass. Molly also had a nice smile and still had a young looking face.

Molly was the mother of the twins, Ally and Cally, who, believe it or not shared the same birthday as Mindy and Me. So, we were all turned 18 that year.

Molly and her two daughters lived in a two bedroom apartment which was not in an very nice neighborhood. So, coming to live in our huge home was like hitting the lottery for them.

Molly had a full time job, but she did not have a college education, so she did not make very much money and had no opportunity to do so in the future.

ALLY:

Ally was one of the twins. Both girls had nice long sexy legs like their mom, but unlike their mom they both had nice firm round tits, not real big, but big enough to have a nice figure. They also both had nice plump asses to go along with those nice legs. They both also had beautiful long blond hair and smiles that could light up a room.

What separated the twins were their attitudes. Ally had an attitude that I think would have annoyed anyone. She was given a nice home to live in with people who were nice to her and she was always angry and uncooperative.

Ally would not clean her room, would not offer to help around the house, did not smile, did not speak nice to anyone, and Ally got poor marks in school which were getting worse.

I sort of fixed Ally thru the use of corporal punishment to make her more livable. Ally became nicer to everyone, got a little better marks, and at least kept her room clean. Ally was not a perfect kid at this point, but she was much better and has become almost tolerable.

However, Ally continued to get poor marks in school I told her that she needed to be trained as a French maid, just like Sabrina. I told Ally that if she did not want to get good enough marks to go to college then she may as well learn a trade, which was being my French maid.

Ally had to wear very short and very sexy French maid

outfits, complete with a collar and five inch high heels, just like Sabrina.

Ally looked absolutely fuckable in her French maid uniforms, but I controlled myself, I think mostly because I did not like Ally, at all, as she was so miserable.

However, even though Ally finished her high school years with all passing marks, overall, Ally's marks were not good enough to get into college.

That was until I changed everything, But, that's another story you will find out about on a Thanksgiving day on the Reform Farm.

CALLY:

When Cally first moved in with me she was a real nice kid and a pleasure to be around. However, in a short while, Molly and I both noticed that Cally was following in the footsteps of Ally and Cally's her attitude was going downhill and even her marks were slipping.

Likewise, thru the use of a couple of hard hairbrush spankings and some corner time, I straightened Cally out right away and Cally has become a nice kid to live with. I thought that Cally was much smarter than Ally and I thought she was better looking also.

Cally was also becoming my friend as she was smart enough to play a good game of chess and could talk to me about things that interested me, like science and math and finance, now, we even discuss sex a little. And, for some reason, for a lesbian, Cally enjoys giving me blow jobs sometimes, always a treat for me.

Unlike Ally, Cally accepted me as being the Boss of the house and Cally would accept her punishments as nothing more than deserved. As I said unlike Ally, who hated me for punishing her.

Thru our growing friendship, Cally, also told me things that I did not wish to hear. Cally, told me that although I was helping her, I myself, was regression into being more of a Bad Boy all the time.

When I thought about the things Cally told me, I could not say that I disagreed with her as I was not as nice of a kid as I was a year earlier. However, as I had no one to answer to, I sort of just told myself that I was having a good time so who cares about the others.

Oddly, however, I did gain respect for Cally for her courage to sort of stand up to me and try to influence me for the better. I wish I had listened to Cally, as my life would have turned out so much better if I did.

At Cally's strange request, Cally was also trained to be a French maid for the summer and she was great. Cally was a good cook, cleaned the house better then Sabrina or Ally, and served everyone with a smile all the time.

Cally also wanted to learn how to give good blow jobs and let me tell you, Cally, became a champion cock sucker. Cally seemed to be able to do whatever Cally wants to do or even says she is going to do.

Cally seems to be a really special person and has become my very good friend.

Now, I have fallen in love with Cally, the lesbian.

SABRINA:

Sabrina was my parents live in maid. I note that she was my parents maid as she did not seem to pay much attention to my needs or my room and this created a growing conflict between Sabrina and me for a number of years prior to this year.

Sabrina was about 26 years old and is a mixture of a South American Indian and black. The result made Sabrina very tall, about six foot tall, a good looking Indian with darker skin then an American Indian but not dark enough to look black.

Sabrina had very nice long and very sexy legs, a real nice muscular looking ass, medium sized tits, big enough to give her a nice figure, but nothing to say wow about. Sabrina also had a nice smile and very nice very long black hair.

I would have gotten rid of Sabrina after the funeral, but in my Moms will she asked that we keep Sabrina. Sabrina had kept my mother happy for many years since Sabrina came to be the maid when she was only 18, about 8 years ago.

I would have gotten rid of Sabrina because even though my Mom acted like Sabrina was part of the family, the fact was that Sabrina was a lousy maid. I use to complain about her all the time and the more I had to say the less and less service I got. It was like Sabrina would punish me for trying to get her to do her job better.

Anyway, my mom and Sabrina were like best friends, so

there was not much I could do, no one seemed to care about what I had to say when it came to Sabrina. Even now, my mom, was reaching back from the grave to try and protect Sabrina from me.

I loved my mom so much and we had such a great friendly and loving relationship, that I could not dismiss her request and agreed with my sister, Mindy, to keep Sabrina on, at least for a while to see if she would shape up. After all, I was now the Boss of the house, she would obey me now, NO?

TONI:

Toni, is a black girl that has become Cally loving girl friend and bed mate. Toni is not gay, as we have discovered Cally is. Rather, Toni, is bi sexual, but spends most of her sexual life with Cally. I have been invited to join them twice and both times were the best sexual experiences of my life.

Toni was about 5 foot 6 inches tall, had long straight black hair, a real nice smile, ample tits and a bigger then proportional ass, as many black girls have. Toni's ass was not fat at all, just bigger then her body frame would show as proportional. Toni had nice thighs, but overall did not have sexy legs.

Toni is a school mate of ours and was expected to die of some blood disease. However, without anyone knowing what we did, Cally and I made arrangements to donate the money Toni needed for a bone marrow transplant directly to some charity and Toni got her transplant and her life was saved and she is recovering.

Additionally, as Toni's family spent so much money trying to save Toni, before Cally and I knew of the problem, they were having their home foreclosed upon as they were not making their mortgage payments. So, Cally and I also paid off the back debt and legal fees so they could keep their home.

No one in their family knew that Cally and I were behind this mortgage payment as Cally took the money directly to the bank and paid it anonymously.

Cally asked why we were going thru so much trouble to make sure no one knew of our charity and I told her because otherwise the family and especially Toni would feel beholding to us and that was not why we were doing it. This way, they just feel some charity took care of them and they were just lucky.

I asked Cally, don't you think your relationship with Toni would be different if she knew that we spent almost $150,000.00 saving her life and bailing out her family home?

Cally recently announced that Toni was doing fine after her transplant and the doctors felt that she could make a full recovery, maybe in about six months.

I also made arrangements for Toni to continue her studies at the same university as Cally, Mindy, Ally, and now Toni. I paid for all of them, except for Mindy of course.

STEVE:

Steve is Molly's husband and Ally and Cally's father. Steve lost his job about 6 years ago and decided to become and drunk and abandon his family as he could not find another good paying job like the one he had.

This is why Molly and Ally and Cally ended up moving in with Mindy and me almost two years ago.

Anyway, I hired a private detective in California to find him.

I went to California to meet Steve after they found him to find out if he wanted to fix his life or remain a drunk forever.

He told me that he would do anything to stop drinking and get a real job and reclaim his family again. I had him sign an agreement and then the detective and a friend of his, that I also hired, followed my instructions and dried him out over the next three months.

Then I gave Steve back to his family last Christmas as a Christmas present that created a room full of tears that one may never see in a lifetime. But, a VERY SPECIAL CHRISTMAS for all.

The cost to me for this Christmas gift was close to $95,000.00.

After Christmas, Cally got Steve a job and he has been doing very well and as far as we all know Steve has not touched a drink and goes to his AA meetings every week.

One week Steve missed an AA meeting and Cally brought him over to the house and strung him up in the back yard and gave him a severe whipping. Steve has not missed a meeting since that day.

THE BOSS:

The Boss is the guy who owns the Reform Farm. The Boss is a very large guy, about 6' 1" and well over 220 pounds or so and all muscle.

The Boss was a very strict man who would never tells you anything twice. You obeyed each and every command with a yes Sir or the Boss would have you severely punished. There was no half ass punishments on the Farm, just severe punishments.

However, the Boss did seem like a fair guy as he did not punish anyone just for fun or to be mean. The Boss was actually the same way I was when I would punish Sabrina or Ally or Cally. I would never punish them for fun or to be mean either, just for disobedience.

PETE AND RICK:

Pete and Rick were the Boss's Forman's and they assigned the work and made sure everybody did their jobs.

Pete and Rick were also the guys that usually punished everyone, although sometimes the Boss would also.

Pete and Rick were both very large fellows, both about 6 foot 4 inches tall and very muscular. Pete was a white guy and Rick was a black guy. They both had muscles on top of muscles and must have weighed about 240 pounds to 250 pounds compared to me at 5 foot 7 inches tall and 127 pounds.

LEMOND UPDATE:

LeMond was the young man that the Boss told me was innocent. Then Cally and I hired a private detective to prove it without the Boss or anybody else knowing.

On September 24th, just after breakfast, two sheriff officers showed up and told LeMond to come with them. LeMond left with the officers but not in hand cuffs, so I thought that was a good sign. I never saw LeMond again after that morning.

A few days later, on September 26th, when I was cleaning up after breakfast and everyone else went to work, Pete came by and told me that the Boss wanted to see me.

I was really nervous as the last time the Boss wanted to see me I ended up getting that severe strapping for a good 30 minutes and had to stand in the corner for one hour a day for 10 days. I did not need any more of that kind of attention. It took all of three weeks for all the welts and bruises to go away from that beating.

As I walked up to the front of the house, I saw the Boss sitting on the patio. The Boss pointed to the chair next to him and told me to sit down, Yes Boss, and I sat down.

Mort, do you remember that day in my office when you were fixing my computer and I told you about LeMond not belonging here as he was innocent and covering for someone. Sure Boss.

Well, Mort, the strangest thing happened earlier today.

Mort, did you see those two sheriff officers that LeMond left with? Sure Boss. Do you know why they were here Mort? No Boss.

Mort, they came to take LeMond back to the courthouse so that he could be released because they caught the real drug dealer, the one that LeMond was protecting.

Mort, that was strange enough, however, the more strange part of the story was that the guy voluntary told the police that in addition to the drugs he was caught with, that he also owned the drugs that LeMond was caught with and LeMond was innocent.

Mort, the guy even proved it to the police well enough so that the district attorney decided to let LeMond go free. Would you know anything about that Mort?

What would I know, Boss, I live here and have no way of communicating with anyone and besides, what would I know of such a world?

Yea, Mort, that's what I thought too, but then I have been doing this job for 20 years now and I have never seen anything like this happen before.

So, Mort, I found it to be more than a coincidence that I mentioned something like that to you one day and in less than two months, this happened. Don't you find that strange, Mort?

Sure do Boss, but good for LeMond, right Boss. The Boss looked over at me and said, Yea Mort, good for LeMond. I did not think that the Boss believed me, but then he did not seem to be smart enough to come right out and ask me if I did something to help LeMond.

Instead the Boss let me get away with answering him with another question, so I really never did answer him. If he had asked me directly, I would not have lied. Lying and me were never friends and I don't think they ever will be.

When you lie, you cannot remember your lies and then you end up lying more to cover yourself. You never have peace of mind that way and when others know you lie, no one trusts you, even when you are telling the truth.

Aright Mort, I just wanted to ask you about that, you can go back to work now. Thank you Boss. OH, Mort? Yes Boss, my computer is still working fine, thanks again. Sure thing Boss, anytime.

Wait Mort, while you are here, there was another thing I wanted to mention to you. Apparently you and Rick have had a problem because of your nigger comment. I know he punished you for that and I was fine with that punishment.

However, Rick is having a personal problem with his brother and is not himself, right now. I have known Rick for many years and he will get thru this, but for now, watch yourself around him and don't give him an excuse to punish you as he may be somewhat too severe because of how he is feeling about his problem with his brother.

So, Mort, do us both a favor and be extra polite and obedient to Rick for now. Thank you for the information, Boss. Alright, Mort, back to work, yes Boss.

CALLY'S THIRD VISIT:

The next day, September 25th Cally was scheduled to come to go over and visit. I was not sure why she was permitted to come before the 30 days were up on October 1st but I was happy to see her sooner anyway. Nevertheless, the reason she came earlier was not good for me.

Cally was brining checks for me to sign and to review the progress for the new house. But, that had nothing to do with the bad news for me that resulted from the early visit.

I was so excited all morning to see Cally that the morning and early afternoon dragged on and on. Finally, I finished cleaning up after lunch like I do every afternoon and I set the tables for dinner and headed to the house to meet Cally.

My walk this day was very pleasant for several reason, first, I really was looking forward to seeing Cally. Second, I was not so ashamed of my panties as Cally knew all about them and actually liked the idea of me in panties.

Third, the plans for the house was exciting to me. Fourth, I had been obedient like Cally told me to be and I was not punished for anything over the past three weeks.

That was a real good thing as my welts from that last

strapping from the Boss were still not all cleared up. I sure did not need any more welts, not now, not ever. I needed to learn to be obedient, I kept reminding myself.

Cally was on the front porch just like last time, waiting for me. Cally jumped up as I approached the steps and gave me a big warm smile and gave me a big kiss as soon I stepped onto the porch. Cally looked great as usual. I wanted to fuck her right there on the porch. But, I also knew that was not going to happen.

Cally stepped back a step and told me to turn around. Cally lowered my panties and could see that I had not been a good boy and pulled my panties back up and turned me around again. Cally did not know about that last beating I got from the Boss, but those faded strap marks were all she needed to see to know, even after 23 days.

Mort, I see that you have been my good boy lately, but what with those faded marks? I told Cally about the Boss finding out about me having him checked out and I told Cally about that long hard strapping that I got as a result.

As I was starting to tell Cally about my punishment, I started to get tears in my eye just thinking about it. Cally, the Boss was real angry with me and he beat me with that big thick strap for about 30 minutes until my ass was so swollen that I could not feel anything anymore.

Then he strapped the back of my legs so hard and for so long there was many places where the skin tore off and my legs were hurting and were sore for two weeks afterwards.

But, Cally, he was still not happy that I was punished severely enough and used a lighter strap on me back and gave me another 50 welts all over my back.

Cally, Then he made me stand in the corner for an hour everyday for 10 days to show off my punished ass and my punished back and my punished legs to all the guys. Cally, as you can see the marks are still not gone and that was over three weeks ago. Cally, the Boss was not happy and made me real sorry I asked you to have him checked out.

Cally, as you can see by looking at my face, I am getting emotional about it as it was just such a long and hard beating, so hard, so painful and so long.

So, Mort, was it worth it, to find out some information and have to take a beating like that? Right now, Cally, I would say, NO! For sure it was not worth it. But, who knows Cally, maybe, someday that information will be worth something worthwhile, who knows? We'll see.

Cally looked at me and was real concerned as to how I was doing. I told Cally that I was fine now, but that was a real bad day when the Boss strapped me. The Boss hurt me like I was never hurt before, Cally. I was sore and I mean really sore for about 10 days after wards.

As you can see, Cally, 23 days later, the bruises still had not all gone away. Cally told me that she was real sorry to hear that, but we had discussed that the Boss might have been real angry if her found out.

Yes, Cally, I know and I took my chances and it did not work out very well for me this time. But, you never can know these things in advance. After all, Cally, look how well it worked out for LeMond. Yea, Mort, I see your point.

Well, Mort, under the circumstances, I will not consider that punishment against you as we took that risk with my consent and it was not like you were disobedient to me. So, Mort, you deserve a nice blow job, as Cally gave me one of her big smiles.

We went in the office and Cally wasted no time at all getting down on her knees and lowering my panties and sucking the cum out of my cock in under two minutes as she usually does. WOW! That was great Cally, I wish I could do something for you. Mort, you just did, now let's move on to some business.

I expected to see all the checks that Cally brought me to sign, but instead Cally presented me with just copies of the checks that "SHE" signed together with a copy of the invoices. I looked thru all the bills and all of the checks and because of the new home, there were many.

I thought that I was going to be annoyed that Cally signed all the checks and paid the bills before I gave my approval of the invoices, but after I saw everything, I had no complaints. I looked at Cally and smiled and said, good job.

Then Cally surprised me, yes I know I seem to say that every time I speak with Cally, but Cally just keeps on surprising me. This time Cally showed me my brokerage statement and there was an extra $65,000.00 in the account over what I expected.

Cally was looking at me with a huge smile of proudest proportions on her face and she told me that she took $10,000.00 out of my account and bought an option on silver and within twenty days cashed out with the $65,000.00 profit for me. What could I say, was she just lucky, or was she smart?

I smiled at Cally and told her that she was not only beautiful that she apparently is really smart as well, what a combination in a women, I added. Thank you for all that you have done for me, Cally. Cally smiled back and told me that it was her pleasure, now let's look at the house plans that she was so excited to show me.

Cally showed me pictures of the progress with the new house. Cally was really excited about them, but to me, I may never even live there. Who knows what is going to be the case in four years for me?

Now, the extra $65,000.00, that was something for me to be happy about. Otherwise, I was just happy to see Cally. I asked Cally about college and she told me that everything was fine and going as planned.

Cally told me that Toni is feeling much better and was getting her strength back and was growing her hair back as well. Cally said the Toni was getting by in college, but was too tired so often and had problems studying as a result, but that should all get better as time goes on.

Cally told me that she warned Ally that since I am not there any longer to monitor her marks that she would still be subject to severe punishment for any failing grades, only from her.

WOW, I sure would like to see Cally spanking the all the white off of Ally's fine ass cheeks. But, I know I will not be there to see it, if it should actually happen.

I told Cally about my new job being the food servant and cleaner. I told Cally that all the guys were use to me and my panties now, but that my name seems to be SISSY now to everyone. Cally, smiled and told me that was fine with her, she really likes me in panties, although Cally added, she did not like the SISSY name.

Cally told me that she would think of a better name for me. I wondered why my real name was no longer any good and Cally needed to think of a new name. So, I asked Cally what was wrong with my real name, Mort? Cally just smiled and laughed and said Mort, that name is not a good sissy maid name.

Sissy maid name? What the hell was Cally taking about I wondered. But, like when Cally says many of the things to me about sissy maids, I just shut up as I guess I don't want to further that type of discussion. I guess I just thought it was better to let her dream?

Then Cally told me that she got a report from the private detective about what was bothering Rick. According to the detective, Rick's 16 year old brother was beaten up pretty badly by two white guys. Rick's brother, Robert, spent two weeks in the hospital and cost the family a lot of money as they had no insurance.

Cally, how much were the hospital bills? About

$32,000.00, Mort. Cally, did they catch the two white guys that beat him up. Mort, the police did not and they did not seem to think it was all that important when our detective asked them about the matter.

So, Mort, I had our detective investigate and he found out who the two guys were. He is waiting to hear from me as to what to do and I wanted to chat with you about it before I told him to act.

Alright, another good job, Cally. Cally, How about if we pay the hospital the $32,000.00 and make sure that they refund the family any money they paid towards the bill already.

Then tell the detective to have the two white guys arrested. Additionally, tell him to make sure he gets them a plea deal so that they will be sent here as there are three empty rooms here. I think Rick would like that, don't you Cally?

Another one of those big smiles that I love from Cally. Alright Mort, I will handle it when I get home.

Alright Cally, what did you find out about Miss Anne, Rick, Pete, and the Boss? Mort, there was nothing worth noting for Miss Anne. The only thing of interest for Pete and or Rick was that they are former Marines.

Now, the Boss, he has been being sued over the last three years over this Farm and how the inmates are treated. Apparently some "DO GOOD" organization which does not believe in corporal punishment is suing him to close the place.

That's interesting Cally. Here's what I would like you to do with that information. Get the file to our lawyer and ask him to find the most respected ex federal judge in that field of law to give you an opinion as to what he thinks of the Boss's case.

How will that help you Mort? Cally, I am not sure, let's see what the answer is and then maybe we will know. Maybe it will mean something and maybe it won't. But, Cally, suppose the Boss loses, will that mean we will all go to a real prison? So, maybe it is important after all.

Alright Mort, I will take care of it and we will see what the opinion will be.

Cally and I went back outside and sat on the front porch. Cally got us a couple of ice teas and some cookies from Miss Anne and we sat on the porch for about two hours and talked about all kinds of things.

One again, Cally stayed for more than the allotted two hours in total. I assumed that after the Boss met Cally that he decided he liked her and therefore did not complain that she stayed too long.

It was almost 5 pm when Cally looked at her watch and told me that she better get going as I needed to get back to work. However, before Cally left, she said, alright Mort, business is over and it's play time again for me now that you have behaved for me since the last time I saw you. AND MORT, you know how it excites me so when you obey me? Yes Cally, I am learning that.

Cally took me back inside to the guest office and gave me another great blow job. Cally looked so sexy there on her knees with my cock in her mouth as she gulped up my cock and sucked the cum out of me for the second time that afternoon.

I thought that Cally may have liked sucking my cock more than I liked Cally sucking it. Maybe, just the same, but that is something that can't be measured so I just enjoyed myself and then it was a long sad walk to the car to see her leave me again.

However, when we got to the car, Cally looked at me and told me that she had one more thing to tell me and I was not going to be pleased about it, so she left it for last. Now I found out why Cally was allowed to visit me before October 1st.

Mort, When we structured the plea bargain, you remember, the agreement that I told you to sign and not read? Yes Cally.

Well, part of the deal was that every three months, Sabrina and Ally would get to come here and watch the Boss punish you. It's not for any current disobedience, it was just part of your overall punishment for you crimes against Sabrina and Ally.

Mort, I know you are getting upset, but stay with me and just listen. Mort, you need to remember, I could not get everything I wanted in the plea deal and something's like these quarterly punishments I did not want. However, in order to get the deal done, Sabrina and Ally insisted on certain things and this was one of them.

So, Mort, I will be coming with them, as more of a guard dog then anything. However, you will be punished in front of Sabrina and Ally in some manner to be determined by them and the Boss.

Mort, I really just wanted you to know that I do not approve and that I could not stop it. And, Mort, before you ask, I did not tell you before now as there was no need for you to worry about something so far ahead that you could not control anyway.

Alright, Mort, give me a big kiss and I will see you on October 1st. OH, Mort, one last thing. Sabrina and Ally don't really know how much I care for you and that is helpful in my ability in keeping them calm and happy about your Farm time as opposed to real prison time, etc.

So, if I act like I don't really care about you all that much when they are around, understand why, Mort. Now, my kiss, Mort.

In spite of how I was feeling at the minute, I managed to cheer myself up a little by making out with Cally for a few minutes and then off she went.

THREE MONTHS VISIT
BY THE GIRLS:

October 1st was my three month anniversary day here at the Reform Farm. I did not sleep well that night as I was nervous about being punished as all the punishments around here are severe and very painful punishments.

However, as the morning moved along, I was getting more and more embarrassed and nervous in advance of Sabrina and Ally seeing me in my panties. Then, they would get to see me punished and get to see me cry as well. I was really hoping that I could take my punishment like a man and not cry, but I just knew that I most likely could not.

I did feel a little like a hypocrite as I thought that it was fine for me to spank or strap or cane or even whip Sabrina and Ally. I loved that I knew they were embarrassed and humiliated in front of others and I thought that was great as well, for me, not them of course.

I loved to watch them cry and suffer in pain and have their bare asses on display for all to see. But, now that the tables will be turned, it just did not seem right to me, to be subject to the same embarrassment and humiliation and have my bare ass out there to be punished for all to see.

Anyway, I was cleaning up after lunch when Pete came to the barn on his horse. Pete dismounted and came into the barn. Rick told me to go and put wrist cuffs on and meet him outside, yes Sir.

I instantly became much more scared, as the time has arrived, as I knew nothing good was going to happen from that point in time. It would be all bad news for me for a while. My tummy started to get upset and I was glad that I skipped lunch, otherwise I may have thrown up.

I put the wrist cuffs on and went outside to meet Pete. Pete told me to hold out my hands, yes Sir. Pete once again hooked my wrists together and then clipped the clip on the end of the rope to my wrist cuffs.

Pete got back on his horse and rode away with me having to follow him as I was being pulled by the horse with my arms stretched out in front of me. As we walked I wondered if anybody else would come to see me like this besides Sabrina and Ally and Cally.

Pete and Pete's horse brought me right up to the front porch of the house and as I got closer it looked like my sister, Mindy, together with Molly and Steve were there also. Great, more people to see me wearing my panties and more people that will get to see me get punished and cry my eyes out, just great.

Nevertheless, Pete brought me right up to the porch and the horse stopped, I stopped and was huffing for air a little as I was somewhat out of breath after a three minute jog in the hot sun. I had sweat dripping down all over my body and my hair was a mess. It was about 86 degrees out that afternoon.

In addition to the six people who came to enjoy my punishment, there were two camera men. As Cally told me, the camera men were going to film my punishments during these every three month "visits" so that everyone I ever insulted, fucked, hurt, teased, called names of, or anything else could watch my punishment over the internet and also enjoy my humiliation. I did not think that I could ever go back to Naples again, as everyone was going to know what happened to me.

I could only assume that this was one big show to show me off to the group to prove that I was being punished even though I was not in prison and I guess, also, just to humiliate me. After all, I was standing there wearing nothing but panties, how embarrassing.

I was really humiliated having Sabrina and Ally see me this way. Not as much for my sister or Molly or Cally. Having Steve there was not something I was expecting and standing there in panties was very embarrassing in front of Steve as I knew Steve was absolutely loving my position in life at that time.

As I thought, since I was the one who use to embarrassed and humiliate and punish Sabrina and Ally, it seemed so extra humiliating to me to be in this position now in front of them.

To make things even worse, my penis started to grow, as it seems to do when I am embarrassed and or humiliated. Sadly for me, it was clearly visible thru my thin clinging wet panties. My panties were only somewhat wet from my sweating, but wet enough to make them extra clingy.

I know that I use to get all excited when I humiliated or embarrassed Sabrina or Ally or even Cally, but now I seem to be getting excited getting humiliated myself in front of others, what was with that I wondered?

This was just horrible, just horrible I thought, but what could I do? Obviously not anything more than Ally could do or Sabrina could do when I did it to them. Except that they did not get erections.

By the time my cock was finished I was standing there in my panties with a full on erection and I noticed everyone looking and whispering to one another making it all that much more humiliating for me. For some reason, Cally seemed to have the biggest smile on her face.

To make matters worse, as matters always seem to get worse around there, even when I thought things could not get worse. Instead of just letting me meet my visitors in my panties, sweaty and dirty, and now with a hard on for everyone's amusement, Pete took his end of the rope and thru it up over that rafter that stuck out about 6 feet past the end of the porch roof.

It was the same rafter that I was left hanging from and that day by Rick when I was all covered in mud as he caned my ass. Pete got off his horse and pulled me up tight again so that only my toes were on the ground and then Pete secured his end of the rope. The only good thing about this position was that my erect penis was at least not facing my "visitors" any more as I had my back to them.

Pete took his horse over and tied it to the hitching post, the same hitching post that I was tied over the first day

I was here when I got that strapping from Pete and Rick and then got that ever so severe strapping from the Boss four weeks ago. As I told you before, it took over three weeks for all those welts and bruises go away so that my ass looked like a nice ass again.

At that point I was thinking that at least I was able to wear my panties today, otherwise my erection would be out in the open for all to see. That would have even been a worse humiliation for me.

I could not believe that I was hanging here being thankful that I was wearing panties in front of all the bitches, funny how things work out sometimes. I mean, up until that minute my panties have been nothing but something that I wish I did not have to wear as the other guys are always calling me a sissy. But at that time I was happy to be wearing panties to cover my rock hard cock in front of my "visitors"

I was still confused as to what kind of visit this was with me just hanging here in my panties all sweaty and dirty with my hands stretched up way over my head while I tried to hold myself up on my toes. I assumed that I was going to be whipped, but I was holding out a little hope that maybe I was just going to humiliated.

If that was the case, then they won, as I was about as humiliated as I have even been in my life. The thought of these bitches, every one of them, sitting there, enjoying an ice tea, while I am dragged to them by a rope attached to a horse and then strung up hang here in front of them with my nice panties showing off my humiliation erection for them.

That was totally humiliating as I could hear them giggling at me even though I could not see them as they were more to my back side, so without turning my head I could not see them.

I guess it was unfair of me to call them all bitches as I had no problems with my sister. In fact, my sister tried to warn me about having sex with Sabrina and Ally and I did not take her advice. Molly was never a problem for me and she appreciated everything I did for her and her daughters.

Cally, as you know, is Cally. So, the ones I called bitches were just Sabrina and Ally who hate me.

My thoughts about the bitches and my total humiliation was interrupted when I heard someone coming up behind me and then rip. The Boss came up behind me and just ripped my panties right off me. So much for that protection.

I never thought that I would miss wearing panties, but today I am. So now my rock hard cock was there for all to see almost like my cock was asking for me to be humiliated like this.

I heard Sabrina start laughing and saying, look at his cock! Do you think that means he is enjoying this? Ally said I hope not, he is here to be punished and I want to see him get punished.

I hung like that for about 10 to 15 minutes. My rock hard cock was becoming not so hard anymore and lost about half of its erectness and was now pointing straight out.

I noticed that all of a sudden the talking on the porch stopped and I could hear someone walking behind me. It was the Boss and he walked around to the front of me and I thought that I was going to pee myself.

The Boss had a long black whip in his hand and he put it up in front of my face as he allowed it to uncoil and said to me that he was going to show all my friends how Bad Boys all really punished around here.

I started shaking from fear, not that I wanted to in front of all my "friends" but I could not control the fear at this point. I mean that whip was about 10 to 12 feet long and looked thick and well capable of putting a real hurt to me.

That combined with the fact that the Boss was a real big strong guy and his smile was telling me that he really enjoys his work, I was almost in tears already. But, at the same time, as soon as my eyes saw the whip, my cock, which was shrinking in size, grew back up to full size to get a better look at it. So, the humiliation just keeps on coming and getting worse all the time.

Ally noticed the reaction in my cock and pointed it out by telling the others, look, his cock likes that whip and they all giggled. The Boss did not give me much time to think about such matters, as he moved around behind me and my back exploded in pain.

The first lash covered my entire back from shoulder to shoulder and the whips tip curled around under my arm pit and bit sharply into my right peck area.

I groaned more by shock then pain, but I can tell you

that I never felt anything like it before. It was actually worse than that punishment cane.

The training cane stings, like bees. The punishment cane stings the same but it also give you a deep down nasty long lasting hurt, sort of like twice the punishment. But the whip felt more like getting hit with an thick electoral cord right in the center of a tight muscle. Except, it was all the way across my back and not in just one small area. Meanwhile, the whips tip provided a serious sting and big welt on the side of my chest.

I did not have much time to get over the first lash when the second one struck just below the first one. The pain was just as intense, however the first lash was still hurting so much and was stinging deep down inside. Now I have two areas hurting just the same.

The third lash was just below the first two, as the Boss worked the whip down my back with the fourth and fifth just below one another. The sixth lash curled around my chest with the tip exploding upon my right nipple which in turn sent electric waves of pain through me. Each lash felt like a hundred bee stings.

I was breathing very heavy just after a few lashes trying to keep my breath and God only knows how many lashes were left. I moaned more loudly after the first few lashes and then I started screaming a little.

At that point I still had some crazy idea that I could avoid humiliating myself further by not crying. but, I had no idea why I thought that was possible as I had cried from every other punishment so far. But it was a thought and a hope.

Lashes seven, eight, and nine, and the tenth hit harder and bit more and I got a much louder and with longer verbal screams, as I burst into tears and screamed and screamed and screamed a little louder. So much for my thoughts about not crying.

If the Boss wanted to assure my visitors that I was being well punished, he sure met his goal as there was no one who could be watching this whipping that thought that I was not almost being killed by the pain as I dangled by my wrist cuffs as I had nothing else to do but hang there and take that whipping.

If the Boss wanted to show everyone that he enjoys his work, there was no question that he met that goal. I could not imagine a punishment worse than this whipping and it showed in my reactions as I screamed after every lash while crying harder and harder and louder with every lash, and he is only up to about 10 lashes with me having no idea how many more were to come.

The whipping continued about one lash every 10 seconds or so, number 11, number 12, through 20 as the Boss worked down the rest of my back to my waist to just above my hips. I was sure my back looked just like a ladder, and with lash 20 I screamed the loudest and the crowd also murmured somewhat.

I was having trouble breathing at this point as my nose was totally clogged with snot from all the crying, so I had to scream and then cry and then try to breath in between.

There was a short break of the whip while I sensed the Boss was moving around, but I could not see him.

Then number 21 struck home, I could tell that the Boss changed sides as he was whipping me from the other side as the tip of the whip would sometimes wrap around the to the front and was now hitting my other side as it snapped making that terrible cracking sound that meant WOW! That really hurt.

The Boss started anew at the top of my back and WOW another Lash brought the same electric shock to my left nipple as the right one experienced and I even felt like a little blood rolling down my chest. The Boss just kept whipping me and whipping me and whipping me, seemly as hard as he could whip me.

Apparently the Boss wanted to punish me and I was being punished like I never thought possible. Apparently the Boss wanted to put on a show for the girls and he was putting on some show. Apparently the Boss wanted to humiliate me and he humiliated me more than I ever thought possible. I never thought that I would ever be in a position like this where I would be crying in front of the girls, but here I was.

I must have received about 40 lashes so far and now the Boss was whipping over areas that already have big fat painful welts on them and that was making the pain even worse. It was hard for me to believe that any lash could hurt more than the previous lashes, but damn if they didn't.

By now the whipping lasted about 10 minutes or about 60 lashes. I knew that I did not have much struggle left in me as I was having more and more trouble keeping at least one of my toes on the ground to give my arms help in holding me up as I was swinging at bit as I struggle after receiving each lash.

The Boss stopped whipping me for a minute while he changed places again. This time he started to whip me again but totally different, not from top to bottom anymore this time. The Boss used no pattern as before and not as much time in between lashes giving me no time to recover as the pace speeded up to only about 5 seconds between lashes.

The Boss also seemed to allow only the last 12 to 15 inches of the whip to strike me at a time instead of maybe 20 to 25 inches as before. This pattern provided even a louder crack as the closer to the end of a whip you get the faster the whip is traveling and therefore makes more sound.

This pattern also provides a bigger sting but not as much deep down pain as before. However, as the Boss was whipping me all over my back, he was whipping over the welts that were already there, making them hurt even worse. Add this to the increased rhythm, the pain was so bad that I thought that I may pass out. I wished I did, but I did not.

These lashes were given at full speed and landed anywhere the Boss wanted, one across, one up and down as opposed to across so that it would crisis crossed the other welts. Having, four, five, six, seven, eight, nine, and ten, the whipping continued and continued and continued with 12 lashes every minute now.

I was basically just hanging by my wrists at that point as I had no strength left in my legs which made by breathing even more difficult. It made my crying more difficult but yet I was still crying just like a little girl who just got a hairbrush spanking from her father.

I did not even seem to have the strength to scream as much and did a lot more groaning, but yet the crying continued with tears all over the place and my snot was dripping and even flying out of my nose in reaction to the next lash.

Three minutes or so later the Boss was up to about 36 additional lashes and the whipping stopped. I was just hanging there by my wrist cuffs with no strength to do anything but cry. My back hurt like nothing that I could ever imagined, the Boss showed my "friends" that I was thoroughly punished and thoroughly humiliated.

I was sure that they had the time of their lives in getting even with me, at least Sabrina and Ally were. I was not sure what the others I thought. I could only hope that it would end here that day. I could only hope that it would end with this whipping and this humiliation that day. I could only hope, as I no longer had any control over anything in my life.

The Boss left me there to hang by my wrists and to cry and cry and whimper some more, as my "friends" were getting ready to leave. As they had to pass me to go to their cars I was feeling a new wave of humiliation as at least before I could not see them seeing me and that was better for me.

The first one to pass me was Sabrina. Sabrina stopped in front of me and just looked at me. Then Sabrina said that this was a good start but my punishment was far from over you big cry baby sissy! No one deserves to be humiliated, whipped, and punished more then you, you pig. Sabrina turned her back to me and walked towards the parking lot.

Ally was the next one to come over to me and just looked at me and said, dirt bag, and kept walking. Molly just walked past me and did not turn around. Mindy, my sister, came over to me she was sorry to see be going thought this and told me to hang in there. I sort of smiled at Mindy and said thank you.

Steve, just walked by and smiled in a sort of laughing manner. but, I know what Steve was thinking. Steve was thinking, how's it feel, you bastard.

Cally was the last one to come by and she stopped and looked at me the longest and had a few tears in her eyes. Finally Cally said, I know that was a real tough punishment for you to take and I know that you are totally humiliated, and I am sorry you are going thru this.

However, Mort, you know that you do deserve to be punished and you know that my panties are soaking wet right now. I need to go Mort, as we discussed, I can't let them think that we are still too friendly, so I will see you when I come back for a private visit.

The Boss left me hanging there for about 15 minutes more after my visitors left and then he let me down. I had a lot to trouble with my balance and the Boss helped me to go and sit on the steps until I thought I could stand.

The Boss went back inside but first told me that when I was up to it I could go back to my room for a hours rest and then I needed to back to the barn and set up for dinner. The Boss said the I did not need to stand in the corner this time or be naked for ten days as I was not being punished for disobedience that I was only being punished as it was part of the deal that the girls would come by every three months and get to watch you get a good hard beating. The Boss added, it just makes Sabrina and Ally feel better to actually see one of your punishments.

I was not sure if that was a good news or bad news. I guess the good news is that I will not need to see them again for three months. The bad news was that I would get to see them again in three months and get another beating even if I had been obedient.

This was not a good day for me, my back was hurting so bad and was so sore and I knew it would be sore for days. That whipping was just the worst and I knew if the Boss wanted to he could have whipped me a lot longer.

I got up and dragged my ass back to my room and laid down and just felt like crying again from the humiliation of getting whipped and crying so hard in front of the girls.

That night while serving dinner several of the guys were taking among themselves about how bad my back looked from that whipping. I heard one guy say that he has never seen anyone whipped so hard before in his three years here.

While some of the bigger and stronger guys were talking

about how they could hear me screaming and crying like a little girl all the way out in the fields. I tried to just ignore everyone and do my job as I could hear Cally in my head telling me again, be brave for me, Mort, be brave for ME!

CHAT WITH THE BOSS:

Just after lunch on October 11, a fine day in Fall day, Pete told me that the Boss wanted to see me. It was 11 days after that long hard whipping and anyone looking at my back could see that the welts had not completely cleared up yet.

Pete looked at me funny this time with a face that showed some puzzlement I thought. What wrong Sir? Mort, you are not in any trouble, the Boss just wants to speak with you.

Mort, the reason I look puzzled is that the Boss never wants to see anyone and this is the third time he wanted to see you and you have not even been here for four months yet.

Sorry, Sir, I can't help you with that, I guess I will go and see what the Boss wants. Maybe his computer is broken again, Sir? Alright Mort, go ahead.

As I was walking down the long path to the house I was thinking that after 10 days, my back was still sore and was still all black and blue, yet faded black and blue.

That was some whipping I got and Cally was right about the humiliation factor. Having Sabrina and Ally and even Steve there to watch me get whipped like that and to see me yell and scream and cry like a little girl. It was just horrible and I now know that I will be punished again like that every three months.

I could feel the pain and humiliation of the next time this far in advance. Add that to the fact that as I spend my time here on the Reform Farm, that the movie of my punishment is being shown to everybody that I went to high school with over the internet.

I will never, for my entire life, be able to face any of those kids as they all know now what I did to Sabrina and Ally and they all know that I was arrested and they all know how I am now being punished. The shame of myself is ever so great. However, I think that is what separates me from a repeat criminal.

I think that I do feel this shame and I realized what I had done was wrong and I even stopped doing it before I was arrested. However, a real criminal does not feel that sense of shame and does not stop by himself before he is caught. I was not sure I was correct, but I guess I was trying to tell myself that I will never be like that again and that I will never get into any trouble again.

I saw the Boss sitting on the porch as I walked up to the house. I walked up the steps and said good afternoon Boss. The Boss pointed to the chair next to him and told me to sit down and as I did he handed me an extra ice tea that he had sitting on the deck. Thank you, Sir, how can I help you?

Mort, something unusual happened again and I was just curious if you knew anything about it. As you know Mort, I do not really believe in coincidences and since you have been here there has been two.

First, Mort, you remember LeMond? Yes Sir. Mort, I told you that he was innocent and that he was coving for someone else? Yes Sir, I remember. Then, Mort, after I told you about LeMond, the real drug dealer was arrested within a month LeMond was set free? Yes Sir, I remember.

Well, Mort, do you remember that I told you about Rick's family problems in an effort to protect you both, as I was concerned that Rick would take his bad feelings out on you and either hurt you or get himself fired, or both. Yes Sir, I remember.

Alright Mort, Now what happened was that somehow Rick's brothers doctors bill that were bankrupting the family have been paid in full by some charity that cannot be disclosed for some reason.

AND, Mort, that is only half the story. Then somehow, the two guys that beat up Rick's brother were mysteriously found and arrested, even though the police were not really looking for them. Apparently they were turned in by a private detective that says he just stumbled across them while working on another case.

Don't you find those two things a strange coincidence, MORT? Yes Sir, I do. Well Mort, there is even more. Now the two guys that beat up Rick's brother are being sent here for their punishment. In fact, I expect them any minute now.

So, Mort, that would be three unbelievable coincidences from just one story. I did not say a word at this point as I was obvious where the Boss was going with this conversation. I just was going to wait this time and see if he knew how to ask the right question where I would have to tell him what he suspected.

So, Mort, I am going to ask you again this time, do you how these three coincidences have occurred? Sir, How could have I had anything to do with things like that? I know nothing about Rick and his brother and I am here, all the time, with no phone or internet to do anything?

Sir, I am complimented that you would think I could be so kind to these guys.

Yea, Mort, you are here all the time and have no phone or internet and yea, what do you know about such things on the outside? Mort, that's the same thing I keep telling myself over and over again. But, Mort, for some reason I cannot seem to convince myself.

Mort, I think you and that Cally are the nicest and smartest young people that I have ever met. I find you both to be most unusual and pleasant to speak with in a place where there really is no one around here for me to speak with.

Do you play chess Mort, Yes Sir. I would like to play you a game or two of chess when you are off duty one night, Mort. Sure, Boss, I would be happy to give you a lesson or two.

Excuse me Mort, a lesson or two. Sure Boss. So, Mort, you have never played me in chess and you know in advance that you will beat me. Sure Boss, and Cally too.

So, Mort, As the Boss smiled at me for the first time

ever, you both think you are that good. Sure Boss. The Boss started to laugh and said, I guess we will see, alright Boss, you just tell me when.

Alright, Mort, I like your confidence, even though I could look at it as disrespectful. But, I know you did not mean it that way. By the way Mort, how is your back feeling? It is still a little sore, Sir. Yes, Mort, I suppose it would be that was a real hard whipping I gave you. Yes Sir.

Mort, I am sort of sorry about having to whip you like that. I never whipped anyone that was not disobedient around here. However, apparently you are the exception to that rule as that was part of your deal with those girls to give you only a four years sentence.

Sir, I understand, it is not your fault that I was a Bad Boy and this is the way I am to be punished. So, Mort, do you don't think I am a mean man for whipping you like that? No, Sir, if it was not you, Sir, it would have been someone else, you were just doing what Sabrina and Ally wanted you to do. That's my fault, Sir, not yours.

Well, Mort, that is a very intelligent and mature attitude of you, I am impressed. Alright Mort, thanks for the chat, you can go back to work now. Thank you too Sir. OH Mort! Yes Sir? The two white guys do not know that Rick is Jose's brother and they don't need to know. Yes Sir!

Just as I was getting up to go back to work the sheriffs van pulled up with the two white guys. Just as I started to leave, Mort, you can stay and watch this, it may be interesting and I understand entertaining for you. Thanks Boss and I sat back down.

THE TWO WHITE GUYS:

The two white guys, Jerry and Greg, got out of the van and walked up on the porch. The two of them could not take their eyes off me as I was sitting there wearing only my panties.

Nevertheless, the Boss told them to take off all of their clothes and they looked at one another and Jerry said here? Right here? Out in public?

The Boss just smiled and said alright not here, I will be right back, you just wait here. The Boss went inside and meanwhile, the two sheriff officers were checking me out and looking at my panties and looking at each other and sort of laughing at me.

I was really humiliated, but what could I do? I blushed all red and just prayed that my cock did not get hard from the humiliation as it sometimes did. However, that seemed to only happen when I was humiliated or embarrassed in front of females.

Although, I did get that erection that time in the barn watching those two other guys get their strapping's. So, this may turn out to be much more humiliating then I first thought?

Within two minutes both Rick and Pete were there. The Boss came out of the house and told the two sheriffs that they could leave. They both looked at me and laughed on their way out. I guess they don't get to see guys sitting around wearing panties too often? Sheltered lives I thought.

Anyway, the Boss told the guys again to take off all the clothes and this time they looked a Pete and Rick and the Boss who were all much bigger than the two white guys and looked at each other and took off all their clothes, including their shoes.

Pete and Rick put a set of wrist cuffs on both guys and then took them over to that roof rafter that hung out from the roof over the yard in front to the porch. Pete strung both guys up, facing each other, with their hands pulled way up over their heads so that their toes only touched the ground just like I was tied up 11 days ago.

The Boss went back inside and came out with a long black whip and tossed it to Rick and told him to handle their introduction to disobedience. As when the Boss told them to take off their clothes and they only asked questions.

I could appreciate their question as I asked the same question on my first hour here and I was severely strapped for my mistake and lack of obedience.

Pete then put a leather strap around the guys waists so that they were really tied together tightly. I assumed that was to stop them from bagging against each other as they were whipped one at a time. However, I sure would not have wanted to be tied to another guy face to face, cock to cock like that.

The Boss sat back down next to me and Rick whipped

those two white guys. Rick whipped them and whipped them and whipped them some more. I don't think that Rick could have had a better time having great sex that day.

Rick took his time and whipped one of them for five minutes, maybe 30 lashes and then whipped the other one for five minutes, maybe 30 lashes as well. The Boss and I sat there and watched Rick whip those two guys for about a half an hour before Rick seemed to get tired of whipping them.

Over all I think they each got about 100 lashes and their backs looked like it was there was not much white left to be found. Nothing but welts on top of welts and more welts.

The two guy were yelling and even screaming a lot during their whippings. They both did a lot of grunting in each other's faces, as they had no choice tied together like they were. However, damn if they did not cry. No crying, no tears, just grunting and screaming.

So, still, I am the only one who cries around there, I guess I am somewhat of a sissy compared to all these other guys, after all.

Yes, I did get an erection watching Rick whip those two white guys. The Boss noticed and looked at me and smiled and nodded his head a bit sort of confirming to himself that he was correct that I would get excited watching that whipping.

When the whipping was over, the Boss told me to get

back to work, yes Boss and I took myself and my panties and my erection and headed back to the barn.

Lucky for me that by the time I got to the barn, my erection was finally gone. Although I did have a pre cum stain on the front of my panties so everyone could tell that I was excited that day for some reason as one time. How embarrassing for me. I was much more self conscious that afternoon then I had been in a while.

NEW CLOTHES:

The next morning, on October 12th, I went to the barn wearing my nice panties and went to work setting up for breakfast. After the guys finished their breakfast and went back to work, Pete came to me with a box in his hand and told me, here, put these on they are you new shoes. I thought that was nice I was getting a new pair of tennis shoes, but I thought that the New Balance tennis shoes I wore were fine.

I thanked Pete an took the box and opened it to find a pair of white five inch high heel sandals. I looked at Pete while he was trying not to burst out laughing at me, Or maybe Pete was waiting to see if I was going to say something instead of obeying him, so he could punish me.

If it were not for Cally, I would have said something and earned myself another beating. But, just as I was about to open my mouth, I could hear Cally in my head saying, Mort, I want you to be obedient!!!!!!!! Just be obedient!!!!!!!!! FOR ME!

I put the box on the table and was about to go back to work when Pete told me that I had to put them on now and that I needed to wear them all the time from now on.

I was not happy, but I could hear Cally in my head, "I WANT YOU TO BE BRAVE AND TO BE OBEDIENT

FOR ME"! So, I sat down and put the five inch high heels sandals on and tried to walk in them. I was a little unsteady, but it did not take long to get use to them as far as my balance went. But, my legs and ankles sure did get sore in a hurry.

As soon as the guys started to come in for lunch I knew that there would be a lot said about my new "SHOES". The guys all teased me pretty good and believe it or not, in a playful way. I guess the guys already thought I was a big sissy so wearing high heels was a natural extension of that persona.

I took me a lot longer to serve everyone as I found out right away that I needed to take much smaller steps. Some of the guys, I think noticed that, and started with the where the hell is my ice tea, what is taking the sissy so long, man sissy is so slow today. Well, you get the idea.

By dinner time the novelty was starting to wear off already with the guys as they had nothing out of the ordinary to say other than to call me sissy as a name, which I have gotten use to hearing and even respond to now.

The next morning Pete came to see me in my room and handed me a pair of shorts. I was almost thankful as I have been just wearing panties for over two months now. However, they were girls shorts. You know the kind, those real short shorts that the girls wear which just barely cover their asses and have something written on the ass.

Mine said "HOT STUFF" So tell me, am I better off

wearing these shorts over my panties or was I better off just wearing the panties. Considering where I am, I guess it did not really matter all that much.

After I put them on and Pete gave me a big laughing smile and he handed me a shirt. Well that I thought that was a good thing, but not so fast, I should have known better. The shirt was one of those midriff tops that ends just past the bottom of your chest so that my whole tummy area was still exposed.

So, my new clothes turned out to be a midriff top of a light green, HOT STUFF green short shorts, and white five inch high heels. What a beauty I was, let me tell you I just looked ridicules.

The guys at breakfast did not have very much to say at all, they were far too busy just laughing their asses off. They were having such a good time laughing at me it made me smile and laugh too.

CALLY'S NEXT VISIT:

It was October 21st the next time Cally came to visit. I had a good report for Cally as I had been the perfect little sissy boy for the farm. I never missed a yes Sir, I never complained about anything, and I worked all day, every day, and kept everyone happy.

I pranced around in my girly clothes and my high heels like I was proud to wear them instead of showing my real feelings of continued deep humiliation.

One day I even heard Pete and Rick talking about my amazing transformation from an entitled little spoiled punk into a respectful, helpful, young girl. Young girl, HUH? That's what they all think of me, as a young girl?

I heard Rick tell Pete that the Boss told them that my amazing transformation was all due to Cally. The Boss told them that Cally changed me like they never could.

That must be some young lady Pete said. Rick said, she is, have you seen her. Yea, but Rick, Pete said, good looks don't change a guy like this overnight, there must be some real substance to her that goes way beyond her good looks. I guess your right Rick said.

It made me proud for some reason that everybody seemed to see the same great things in Cally that I saw, she sure was growing into a terrific and very, very special young lady.

As I was walking to the house that afternoon I was realizing how long it took me to get anywhere in these five inch high heels that I had wear all the time.

It's been over 10 days now and at least I was pretty use to them by then. I learned to walk in them in a few days with ease. However, the entire first week my calf's and ankles were sore as I was not use to such heels.

10 days later I could wear them all day without much trouble, but, as I said, it takes longer to do everything when you can only take small steps and need to keep your feet under you to maintain your balance. It was taking me about three short steps in these heels for every one step in my tennis shoes to move the same distance.

So, serving in the barn takes a lot longer and walking down to the house was taking a lot longer. However, and I hate to admit this, I really liked the high heels as I felt sexy in them and they made my ass wiggle a little and all the guys seem to like me that way. I was not sure what to make of all that, so, I just told myself that I had no choice and that is the truth anyway.

I met Cally On the porch at 2 pm and the first thing Cally did as I walked up to her was tell me to turn around. I did so and Cally told me to lift my shirt and I did so. Fine, Cally said, now drop the shorts and panties. I did so and Cally told me to pull them up and have a seat.

Cally smiled at me and said, Mort, I see that you have

been a good boy and you have obeyed me. Mort, this is about six weeks now that you have been obedient and I appreciate it. I don't like them marking my stuff. I was wondering when I became "HER STUFF", but I was sure alright with me. I sure did not mind being HER STUFF!

Mort, I really do like your new clothes. Little by little you are becoming my girlfriend, as Cally was grinning at me with that big smile of hers that I enjoy seeing so much.

Cally? Yes Mort? Are you telling me that I am dressed like this being humiliated out of my mind at your request? Cally smiled and laughed a bit and, yes Mort.

I felt so disappointed as this was Cally that was treating me so poorly and not the Boss. BUT, Why Cally? Why? Because I like you this way, Mort, It excites me and pleases me. And, because you are never going back to being that Bad Boy, you may as well learn to be my girlfriend now, sooner than later, that's why Mort.

BUT, CALLY? As I started to get upset. THEN, I got that stern face from Cally, the stern face that made me feel so submissive and obedient and yes, excited me too.

MORT, NO BUTS! Now, you just calm down and you will dress the way I want you to dress from now on, do you understand me, Mort? From now on Mort, you will always dress to please me, END OF DISCUSSION! MORT!

MORT, DO YOU UNDERSTAND ME? Yes Cally. Good Mort, because one more word out of your mouth about how I have you dressed will result in you being punished. DO YOU UNDERSTAND ME MORT? Yes Cally. Well, I guess Cally ended that conversation.

Alright then Mort, on a different subject, I wish to tell you again that I did not like having you whipped like that, but that was one of the things that Sabrina and Ally insisted be included in the plea agreement, so I needed to allow it. So, Mort, that will be something we will both have to live with for a while longer. All I could do was smile to Cally. I really had no comment.

Alright Mort, let's go in the office as my mouth has been missing being filled with that nice hard cock of yours. Since you have been obedient I will have my treat today.

As Cally usually does, she got down on her knees and took my entire hard cock into the her lovely mouth and sucked the cum out of me in under two minutes. Odd, I thought, while Cally was being so stern with me I got that raging erection. It was almost as if I liked being talked to in the manner?

I pulled my panties and shorts back up and Cally showed me some updated pictures of the new house and we went over some bills that she paid. Cally does not bring me copies any more, she just shows me the check book and answers any questions I have, which is rare. I never seem to question anything Cally decides to do.

Cally showed me my financial statement and I looked at Cally and just said really? Yes Mort, When oil was down to about $80.00 a barrel I took $10,000.00 of you money and bought an option and I just sold my option when oil got back to $100.00 a barrel. So, yes Mort really, I made you an extra $200,000.00. Cally, really? Yes Mort, now aren't you happy I wanted to take care of you money in lieu of that banker.

Well, yea Cally, that is a great job. Cally, yes Mort? Do you not want some of this money? Mort, I have everything in life I could want, well almost, so no, if I want some money I will take it then, but thanks for asking.

So Cally, now that you have made me an extra $265,000.00 this year I will be at about $6 million at year's end, right? Yea, Mort, that's the way I figured it also.

Alright Mort, it is a beautiful day outside, let's go out and sit on the porch and chat out there. Cally and I got some ice tea from Miss Anne and went out and sat on the rocking chairs on the porch and we chatted about many other things that day.

A while later Both Rick and Pete came by and went into the house. I was convinced that they just wanted to get a look at Cally, and that was alright with me, I was proud just to be able to sit next to her.

It was getting late and Cally was getting ready to go, but Cally told me to come inside again with her first and took me into the guest office again and closed the door and pushed me up against the inside of the door and started making out with me like she had never been kissed before.

I kissed her back like I never kissed any other girl and loved every minute of it. Cally then dropped to her knees and yanked my shorts and panties down and took my cock in her mouth again and within a minute Cally was again gulping down my cum again.

Cally got up and told me, that's what happens to good boys, so Mort, you continue to obey me. I smiled and walked Cally to the parking lot where I got more great kisses.

Mort? Yes Cally? two things, first, I have received permission from the Boss to visit you more often than only once a month for now on.

Two, Mort, and this is very important to me. I want you and expect you to be totally obedient around here. I do not expect to come back here and see any punishment marks on you, I want you to be my good "girl". If you disobey them, Mort, you disobey me, AND THAT WILL NOT PLEASE ME, MORT!

Do you understand me, Mort. Yes Cally. Good Mort, and off she went.

SPANKING:

It was November 2nd and I was looking forward to seeing Cally again in two days, on the 4th.

I had continued to be a good "girl" for Cally and I wore my slut clothes everyday while I worked all day, three meals a day in that barn, serving and cleaning after all the guys breakfast, lunch, and dinner.

I always showed up on time, I always got my job done very well, I was always very polite to everyone, and I accepted the fact that my name was now SISSY.

I had a whole different attitude towards my slut clothes since Cally told me that she was responsible for them and that she liked me in them as I looked more like a "girlfriend" to her.

So, I did not mind wearing them so much as before, However, the humiliation factor is still always there, I just accepted it better and thought that I was pleasing Cally, which helped ease my mind somewhat.

However, this day at breakfast, those two white boys were teasing me about being a sissy and one of them, Jerry, said that he was available to fuck that hot chick for me, as I was probably worthless to her with my little dick. Obviously he was taking about Cally and I threw a cup of hot coffee in his face as he was not going to disrespect Cally that way.

Jerry jumped up to hit me, but the two guys next to Jerry jumped up and held Jerry back. Rick was over there in a flash and I told him the truth about what happened. Jerry said he was just having some fun, but Rick reminded him that direct teasing like that is prohibited and Jerry will be punished.

Rick, looked over to me and told me that I should also know better, words are just words and that I would be punished also.

Rick told Jerry to take his shorts off and go and stand in the corner and for me to come with him. I assumed that I was going to get a strapping or a caning, but I was wrong.

Rick moved a chair over in the doorway opening to the barn and then went over to a cabinet and pulled out a large wood hairbrush. I was not sure but I thought it looked like the one that I used to spank Sabrina and Ally and Cally.

How ironic I thought if it was the same on that now I would be the one getting spanked with it, only here in front of all these guys. My humiliation factor was soaring as I could feel all the heat in my red face.

Rick went over to the chair and sat down and called me to his side. Rick reached over and pushed my shorts down my legs to the floor. Then Rick humiliated me to no end when he put his finger tips in the waist band of my panties and slid them down to my knees.

I guessed this was the same degree of great humiliation that the girls would feel when I took their panties down for a spanking with everyone else in the family watching them. Not so exciting when it was me that was getting embarrassed the same way and about to get the spanking.

Rick tapped the hairbrush against his lap and looked at me and told me that I know what to do and I said yes Sir and laid over Ricks lap. Rick started spanking me right away with real hard hairbrush spanks that had me kicking my legs and yelling OUCH!!!!! right away.

Rick was spanking me real hard and real fast, about one spank every two seconds with no pattern other then pain and pain and more pain. As Rick was spanking me so hard I kicked my panties off and screamed and yelled and acted just like one of the girls acted when I spanked them.

I could not believe how much the hairbrush was hurting my ass. Rick was spanking me very hard as it was hurting far worse than I had expected and all I could do was kick my legs a little, bounce my head up and down and yell like the big sissy I was.

I could not believe that a spanking could hurt this much and I guess I was leaning how much I was hurting the girls when I would spank them like this. Although, I was never a 250 pound muscle man and I thought that may be helpful in delivering such a painful spanking.

I was trying to be tough and take it like a man so that I would not humiliated myself in front of all the guys any more than I had too. However, that thought was not helping and the more spanks Rick delivered the more

I moaned, ouched, kicked my legs, started to sob, and got a runny nose.

Rick seemed to want to put on a good show for all the guys as he usually does and Rick also had that other reason to spank me as hard and as long as he could. If you Remember, Rick hates me for calling him a nigger, well to be fair to Rick, that was really, "fucking nigger", some mouths back.

SPANK, SPANK, SPANK!!!!!!!!!!!!!!!!!!!!!!!!!!!!! I had snot dripping out of my nose, I could not see anything clearly as the tears were dripping from my eyes as the spank total climbs towards 30 or 40 or maybe 50.

Rick is getting into a nonstop rhythm of SPANKING, SPANKING, SPANKING!!!!!!!!!!!!!!!!!!!!! I did not think I was going to be able to sit down for a month, and damn if I would ever do anything wrong again I thought. I forgot all about trying to be brave and take the spanking like a man as I was taking it just like a little sissy I was. The humiliation was much worse than I had imagined.

The humiliation was so, so bad, everyone of those guys that I see and serve everyday was there watching me get an over the knee bare ass hairbrush spanking, just like I was a little kid. After all, I sure cried like I was a little kid.

Rick spanked up one side of my ass and down the other side and SPANKED and SPANKED and SPANKED me some more. Rick SPANKED up and down and back and forth from cheek to cheek. I thought that I was crying just as hard as I did when the Boss whipped me.

I wanted the spanking to stop so badly but what could I do, except lay over Ricks lap and take my long hard spanking in front of all the guys.

The SPANKING, SPANKING, SPANKING, SPANKING, SPANKING!!!!!!!!!!!! continued. At that point I must have received around 100 really hard spanks but little did I know Rick was only half way through my spanking. I was crying so hard and kicking my legs up and down and Rick just pounded me even harder with that hairbrush.

The SPANKING continued as Rick was delivering a hard spank about every two seconds, so that SPANKING had been going on for about three to four minutes at that point. They were some of the longest three or four minutes of my life. I was no longer thinking about the guys watching me ass get the SPANKING of my life.

I was no longer concerned about sitting down again, I was not thinking about anything except the severe pain in my ass as the Rick just continued to SPANK, SPANK, SPANK!!!!!!!!!! SPANK!!!!!!!!!!!!!! SPANK!!!!!!!!! until I had no struggle left in me and all.

Finally, I just laid limp across Rick's lap and took the SPANKING!!!!!!!!!!!!!!!!! I was crying so hard I was surprised that I did not run out of tears.

Finally the spanking of my life came to an end, after about 200 maybe 250 spanks later and about 8 minutes in time. I had no strength to get off Rick's lap and I just laid there.

I continued to cry and try to get air though my mouth as

my nose was clogged and dripping with more snot. Rick allowed me to remain there over her lap for a minute or so and then Rick helped me off and told me to go stand in the corner, yes Sir, I chocked out thru my crying.

As I got up I could see all the guys looking at me like watching me get that spanking was some of the best entertainment they ever seen and I was sure that it was. I had no idea where my shorts or panties were as they flew off early on during the spanking as I was kicking my legs.

However, I did not need them right away anyway. Shorts and panties were not a requirement for standing in the corner in front of all the guys with my freshly spanked ass on display.

Yes, I know that all the other guys were punished several times and also had to stand in the corner showing off their punished ass or back or both. However, no one else got an over the knee spanking like I just got, like I was a little kid. Just when I thought that nothing else around here could embarrassed me or humiliate me anymore Rick proves me wrong.

Anyway, there I was standing in the corner. Rick called Jerry over and took Jerry and put the wrist cuffs on him and made him stand in front of one of the wood roof support posts that were throughout the barn.

Rick tied Jerry's hands high up over his head and then used a wide leather strap to secure Jerry's waist to the post so Jerry was not going anywhere.

For the next 10 minutes all that anyone could hear in

that barn was Jerry grunting, sometimes very loudly. The only other sound in the barn was the constant CRACK!!!! CRACK!!!! CRACK!!!!! CRACK!!!! CRACK!!!! CRACK!!! Rick was strapping Jerry across the back and Rick was strapping him hard, so hard, with a big long thick strap.

I think that Rick hates Jerry more then he hates me, after all, Jerry beat up Rick's bother real bad for no reason. I just Called Rick a nigger. So, this had to be a great day for Rick as he got to humiliate me and spank the snot out of me and now he was strapping Jerry with such enthusiasm.

CRACK!!!!!! CRACK!!!!!!!! CRACK!!!!!!!! CRACK!!!!!!!!!! CRACK!!!!!!!!! On and On and On for about 10 minutes and maybe 100 LICKS in all. the room was quiet as I think the guys were even surprised at the viciousness in which Rick was strapping Jerry.

When Rick finally let him down and sent him back to the corner, I could see his back and it was just one big welt. I could not see any white skin, just big huge welts on top of welts.

When my corner time was up Rick told me to get dressed. Rick told me that from now on I don't have to be naked anymore for 10 days after I am punished. Rick said that wearing my girly clothes, as he called them, was punishment enough.

However, I needed to stand in the corner for 30 minutes a day for the next 5 days at breakfast time. While I am standing in the corner, I needed to do so with my shorts around my ankles and my panties around my knees, so my spanked ass will still be on display. Rick was correct, that was more humiliating then being totally naked. Standing in the corner showing off my panties and spanked ass like that.

CALLY VISTS ON NOVEMBER 4TH.

It was the morning of November 4th and I was very nervous and also very excited all morning as I knew Cally was coming at 2 pm to visit with me. Obviously I was excited as I miss Cally so much and I am so happy to see her every single time.

I was nervous as I knew Cally would be disappointed due to my disobedience that resulted in my spanking two day ago. So, I also guessed that I would not be getting a blow job during this visit.

I walked from the barn to the house just before 2 pm and Cally was not there on time for the first time. I was very concerned that Cally may be angry with me because of my disobedience and decided not to come that I almost started to cry.

As I walked up on the porch hoping that perhaps Cally was waiting inside, the Boss came out the front door and told me that Cally was running a little late and that I should wait for her in the corner.

The Boss pointed to the same corner I stood in one my first day at the Reform Farm when Cally was inside introducing herself to the Boss. Yes Sir, and I walked towards the corner and stood there.

Then I heard the Boss say, Mort, the shorts. I was really

afraid of that as I had to lower my shorts to my ankles and my panties to my knees and stand in the corner like that until Cally gets there and my spanked ass will be the first thing Cally see when she shows up.

I felt so bad disobeying Cally and now I was so much more embarrassed standing in the corner waiting for her. I started to get tears in my eyes as I knew that I was going to have a problem looking into Cally's eyes when she arrived. Nevertheless, I could not let that guy talk about Cally like he did. I did not know how else to handle it.

Cally arrived about 15 or 20 minutes later and as she walked up the steps to the porch I heard her say I see my girl has been a naughty girl. Cally told me to pull up my panties and shorts and turn around.

As I did Cally came over to me and told me to tell her how and why I was spanked. I told her the story and as I told her about how humiliated I was to be spanked like a little kid and how I cried like a big baby in front of all the guys, I could not contain my humiliation and started to cry right there in front of Cally.

Cally actually looked at me and smiled. Mort, I understand why you threw the coffee at Jerry and in a way I think it was very sweet of you to protect me in such a way.

However, Mort, those feelings are secondary to the obedience I expect from you and unless there is some type of an emergency, there is never any reason or any excuse that permits disobedience. Mort, if anybody should understand that, you should.

So, Mort, there will be no blow jobs for you today and I am going to cut my visit short as I don't expect to come here and find any punishment marks on you as I have told you, do you understand me? Yes Cally.

Cally told me to sit down and she went inside and got some ice teas and came back and we sat on the porch and talked about all kinds of things, but nothing specific as Cally really did not have bills or news for this visit.

Mort, do all the other guys around here get punished a lot or are you the only disobedient one? Cally, there is hardly a week that goes by where one of the guys does not get punished for something. I don't usually get to see their punishments as they are usually here at the house when everyone is working.

However, everyone knows when anybody gets punished as they all have to stand in the corner in the barn during one meal a day for three to five days after their punishment showing off their welts. Then, they are kept naked for 10 days just like I was so everyone could see their welts all the time as they were to be humiliated by being naked.

Alright Mort, I was just curious. However, Mort, I don't care about the others, I only care about you and I expect you to be totally obedient, do you understand me Mort? Yes Cally.

Cally, you did not mention anything about your midterm grades, I know that they should have come out by now, no?

Sure, Mort, we got them a few days ago. Mindy and I

both got 4 A's and one B, in math. Toni, who is feeling much better was able to get by with all C's this time. However, now that she is feeling better she should do better, as you know Mort, Toni is smarter than C's.

However, Toni does know the house rules about marks, so I sure she will do much better. Cally, what do you mean the house rules? Mort, your house rules, the same rules you had.

You don't think that just because you are not there that I would put up with any bad marks do you? I just smiled in somewhat of a surprise as I never thought that Cally would continue my rules about grades.

Sure, Mort, that brings me to Ally. Ally got 3 B's and one C and a D in math. Mort, I spanked the snot out of Ally the other night and told her if she fails any more classes that in addition to being punished, she will lose her car too.

WOW! Cally, I had no idea. Mort, you were right in treating us that way with our grades, look what you did for me. I am everything I am proud of today because of you and the way you punished me and the way you rewarded me and yes that will continue in your house with or without you being there.

Yes Mort, and I guess I should tell you that I did get a big thrill, I mean I got real excited when I had Ally stand next to me while I sat on the spanking chair and put my hands up under her skirt and lowered her panties, just like you use to do.

And, Mort, by the time I was finished spanking Ally

and making her ass turn all red and then dark red and then purple and then black and blue and as I listened to Ally cry and scream and cry some more. I was so excited Mort, that I had Toni lick my pussy afterwards for me for an half hour to five orgasms. It was great Mort, just great!

However, Mort, that does not apply to Sabrina. I told Sabrina that she knows exactly what I expect of her and if she does not like it or does not perform, I will just fire her as I have no patience for her. After all Sabrina is not family, Mort. Since that day, Mort, Sabrina, overall, has been pretty good and we get along fine.

However, Mort, I do not make her wear those French maid dresses as they remind my too much of your Bad Boy behavior. But, Mort, you know how much I liked Sabrina and Ally in those French maid dresses, so in a way I was sorry to let her stop.

For now, I let her wear a more plain and formal maid outfit, but still with a short hem line and 4 inch high heels. Mort, I guess I will just need to wait until you are my sissy maid to have my maid in those French maid clothes again that I like so much.

There Cally goes again telling me that I will be her sissy maid one day. That is some imagination Cally has, why does she keep saying stuff like that to me I wondered?

Cally and I started to chat about other things, But after only one hour, Cally told me to go back to work and she was going inside to see the Boss. MORT! Yes Cally. I know I am repeating myself, but I expect complete obedience for my next visit and I don't want to hear any stories, just obedience, got it, Mort? Yes Cally, alright Mort, go on now. Yes Cally.

As much as I enjoyed Cally's visit, I did not even get one kiss that time. I guess Cally is real serious about that obedience stuff.

I guess I could not complain, everything Cally does for me or says to me is for my own good and it always has been and I knew it.

REFORM FARM THANKSGIVING:

I woke up at my usual time and went to the barn as I did everyday for breakfast. I understood that Thanksgiving on this farm in not a holiday, it is just another working day.

That was fine with me, I had no one to share Thanksgiving with that year anyway. It was just another sad and lonely day of work for me and I had still had almost 43 months of this fun to go, so I may as well get use to it and go to work.

I took my usual long walk to the barn in my five inch high heels that made the trip a very slow and hip wiggling sexy experience for any of the guys to enjoy as they seem to those days. I guess I was just nothing more that something for them to laugh at in a place where nothing was very funny.

After breakfast that morning Pete came over to me and told me that I did not need to set up for lunch as everyone would be eating elsewhere. Elsewhere? Yea Mort, look outside.

Pete and I walked over to the barn door and there was a big truck outside and a bunch of guys setting up a big tent. Pete told me that we would be eating lunch under the tent later today. I had no idea why and Pete did not know either. Pete just told me that was what the Boss told him and the Boss did not tell him why.

When I was finished cleaning up after breakfast and all the dishes and everything else were washed and put away I was told by Pete that I could go back to my room and relax until lunch time.

As I walked back to my room I was looking at the area where the tent was put up and it looked to me that it was 3 or 4 times larger than it needed to be to have enough room for the 14 of us prisoners and the four others. Pete, Rick, The Boss, and Miss Anne.

But, hell, it was none of my business. However, when I got to my room I found on my bed a real pair of long pants, a nice shirt, and my new balance tennis shoes. There was a note from the Boss that said, for today Mort, get dressed.

I was happy to get dressed, but still had no idea why. My feet actually felt funny in my tennis shoes after wearing nothing but those five inch high heels all day for over a month now.

I sat outside of my room in a chair and read a book for a while and then noticed all the other guys coming to their rooms. Like me they all found a nice pair of long pants and a nice shirt to wear.

They all gathered outside their rooms and were discussing what was going on as the Reform Farm never recognized any holidays before, not even Christmas. They all passed by the big tent while coming back to their rooms, but we could not see over there from where our rooms were to see what was going on.

Around 2 pm Pete came by and told everyone to come with him and we all went to the big tent. As we walked over there I noticed a lot of cars in and around the driveway. So many cars that most of them were parked on the grass.

Just as I got near the tent I saw Cally and I started to cry a little and as I looked at Cally, she too was crying lightly. We hugged and kissed and I just wanted to squeeze her all day long.

If nothing else happened that day other than me getting to sit next to Cally and enjoy a meal with her I would have had a great Thanksgiving, considering the circumstances, of course.

Cally asked me if I had been a good girl since last time she saw me and I confirmed that I had been. That got me a nice smile and a nice kiss and Cally telling me that that made her happier.

I saw all the other guys also hugging many other people, so I assumed that everyone had relatives who came that day to enjoy a meal with imprisoned kin. For 14 inmates, there must have been almost an hundred people there altogether.

Cally and I went into the tent and I also saw Mindy and Molly and even Ally came. Ally's attendance really surprised me as why would she come to spend any time with me I thought?

Regardless, We all sat down to enjoy Thanksgiving dinner together, Ally sat next to Molly so that she was not sitting near me. I asked Cally if she knew anything about dinner as I was told that they never celebrate any holidays around here?

I had no idea as to why I thought that Cally would know anything about this, but then I know Cally. Cally, told me that the last time she visited she told the Boss that this would help the moral of the guys as family was all those guy really had in life.

Mort, the Boss told me that they could not afford such things, so I told him that I would pay for everything and set up the entire event and he agreed to it, so here we are.

Mort, I would have done anything to spend this time with you, I miss you so much. Cally and I both had tears dripping down our cheeks again. I could do nothing but smile, I just love being near Cally, she always made me feel so complete. Without Cally, I always felt empty.

Later after we all ate and were taking about the new house and several other things. Cally said, Mort, I have a question for you. I just looked at Cally, but I also noticed that Molly and Mindy and even Ally got real quiet and listened.

Mort, as you know, we all wondered how Ally got into the same university as you and I based on her marks. Other kids I know had to go to community college as they were not accepted to the university and many of them had better marks than Ally.

Mort, I know we had discussed this in the past and you just told me the school had a couple of openings and that you were just lucky to be there in the right day to get Ally signed up. I did not say anything as there was really no question there.

Well, Mort, the other day I was over in the tennis court area and I saw a plaque on the wall of the new Tennis building and the plaque said the new tennis building was possible because of a donation of $50,000.00. by you, Mort.

Now, Mort, that donation was made the day before you told me that story about Ally being accepted was just good luck.

So, Mort, the real truth was that after Ally gave you a hard time for almost a year and Ally hated you all that time you paid them $50,000.00 to accept Ally into the university, did you not? I just looked at Cally and had no choice but to say, Yes Cally.

Well, now we have become a real spectacle as Cally was crying as she was so proud of me. Molly was crying and Mindy was also crying. I had tear running down my face just from watching Cally cry. But, the biggest surprise was that Ally was crying.

The Boss came over as he thought something was wrong as everyone else in the tent became quiet and just watched to see what all the crying was about. The Boss asked what was wrong and Cally held up her hand to wait and the Boss waited until Cally calmed down.

Cally explained to the Boss why she was crying as she was

so happy with me and she told him the donation story that actually did buy Ally's way into the university.

Cally told the Boss that I never told anyone about it and that I did this in spite of how Ally treated me.

The Boss looked at Cally and said that is an interesting story. The Boss looked at me and told me that he guesses Cally was right about me after all.

Later that afternoon after everyone went home the Boss called me over to him. Mort, I would venture a guess that if I asked you before today if you knew anything about how Ally got into college, you would have just asked me what could you have done to accomplish such a feat?

After all, Mort, you would have told me that they would not have paid any attention to anything a young fellow like yourself would have had to say on that matter.

I just looked that the Boss and told him, that sounds about right, Boss. The Boss asked me that theoretically speaking, if I was to have helped LeMond or Rick's brother, why would it be that I did not want anybody to know.

Theoretically speaking, I told the Boss was that my theory would have been that when someone gets such a gift, they then feel that they own the gifter something. By being anonymous, they never feel that way and that makes the gift even better.

So, in this case, Mort, you did this nice thing about 18

months ago and Cally just found out about it on her own now? Yes Sir.

The Boss just looked at me and said, alright Mort, alright, you can go. Oh, wait, Mort. I do have one more question for you. You did an over the top nice thing for Ally, yet she did not seemed happy to find out the truth as did the rest of your family. why?

Boss, Ally hated me since the day she moved in with me as I was rich and she had nothing and she just had a bad attitude about everything in life. However, Ally is also one of the two who I abused causing me to be here. So, Boss, I guess I can understand her bad feeling towards me.

But, Mort, you did it for her anyway, even though you knew how she felt about you. Boss, I always try to do the right and be generous because it is the right thing to do, not because I hope that the people will like me for it or appreciate me for it, so it really does not matter.

What does matter, Boss, is that Ally is there getting a good education and her life opportunities will be much better as a result. Boss, when I did not follow those "GOOD LIFE" principles, I ended up here.

THE WORST AND BEST DAY OF MY LIFE:

It was December first, and I had been wearing my new clothes for over a month at this point and in spite of the continued comments from the guys I managed not to mind all that much by being their daily serving maid for breakfast, lunch, and dinner. Nevertheless I was not happy, as you can imagine, being dressed everyday as a 20 year old whore out looking for some cock.

However, since I was dressed like this because Cally wanted me to be dressed like this, I thought there was no hope in getting any real clothes to wear. However, want I really wanted was my computer.

So, I asked Pete at breakfast if I could see the Boss, after all, the Boss was a business man and should understand the persuasion of a business offer. I mean, it was not like I was going to ask him to let me go, I just wanted my computer.

Pete told me at lunch time that I had an appointment with the Boss at 2 pm. I thanked Pete and went about my business of serving the guys and cleaning up after they went back to work.

I finished cleaning up everything after lunch and headed down to the house at 1:50 pm. The Boss was waiting on the front porch having an ice tea and told me to come on in and took me to his office and closed the door.

So, what's on your mind sissy? See, even the Boss calls me sissy, I don't even think he knows what my real name was anymore. Well, Sir, as I did say nervously, it's about my computer, Sir. What about your computer, sissy? Well Sir, I.... I just wanted to.... to ask if there was some way that I could get my computer back, Sir?

What do you mean, some way, has something changed as to your status around here? Well, Sir... I.... I was thinking that I pay a lot of money to stay here on this farm and I was.... wondering.... if there was some additional amount that could help me get my computer back, Sir?

I think.... I think... I just made a mistake as the Boss got noticeably upset and turned all red in the face and just looked at me with these big eyes and finally said, sissy do you realize that you just committed a crime for trying to bribe me?

I became instantly frightened as I figured I was in trouble again, especially after I tried so hard to stay out of trouble for the past thirty days. I mean my bruises from that spanking I got from Rick finally disappeared last week and now I will probably be getting another beating. Cally is going to be upset with me again and I can't stand it when Cally is upset with me.

Just then the Boss started yelling at me, YOU LITTLE PIECE OF RICH SHIT!!!!!!!!!! YOU THINK THAT YOU CAN COME IN HERE AND THINK YOU CAN BUY ME!!!!!!!!!!! YOU COME INTO MY OFFICE AND INSULT ME WITH YOU MONEY!!!! WELL SISSY, YOU MADE A BIG MISTAKE, A BIG MISTAKE!!!

I never heard the Boss yell before and I was finding it

very scary. Just then the Boss got up out of his chair and came around the desk and I thought that he was going to hit me and I think he wanted too.

But, he only grabbed me by my shirt and looked into my eyes and told me that he would just love to beat the shit out of me, but instead he pushed me into the couch.

YOU FUCKING LITTLE RICH BOY, THINKS HE CAN BUY ME!!!!!!!!!! As the Boss continued to be physically upset with me. WELL YOU LITTLE SHIT, DO YOU KNOW THAT I COULD SEND YOU TO PRISON FOR AN ADDITIONALL FIVE YEARS FOR BRIBERY?????????? DID YOU KNOW THAT YOU LITTLE PIECE OF SHIT, YOU MAKE ME SICK!!!!!!!!!!!!!!!!!!!

The Boss seemed to calm down a little and looked at me for a minute and told me to go and get the wrist cuffs and bring them back here. I got up slowly and said yes Sir. I went out to the porch and got the wrist cuffs that were hanging on the railing and brought them back to the Boss.

The Boss still looked very angry as he grabbed the wrist cuffs from me and told me to turn around and fixed the wrist cuffs behind my back and then grabbed my arm and very roughly took me back out to the porch and put me in the corner by the railing that faces the parking lot.

The Boss yelled at me, YOU STAND IN THAT CORNER UNTIL THE PRISON VAN GETS HERE TO TAKE YOU AWAY, YOU GOD DAMN PIECE OF SHIT!!!!!!!!!!!

I was never so scared in my life. Even when I got arrested I never thought that I would be going to prison as I kept telling myself that I did not do anything wrong so why should I go have to go to jail?

But, now, the Boss says he is sending me there and that I would get an additional 5 years for trying to bribe him. I got a few tears in my eyes as I just stood in the corner and waited for the prison van.

The more I thought about it the more sick I started to feel. Then for some reason I thought about not being able to see Cally anymore, and I felt so sick I threw up over the railing and fell to the floor as I just did not have the strength to stand up any longer.

I think Miss Anne heard the thump when I hit the deck and she came out of the house to check on me. Miss Anne got a towel and wiped my face of the vomit that was leaking out of my mouth and got me a glass of water and gave me a few sips and helped me get back on my feet.

I managed to get a thank you out to Miss Anne and she told me I was welcome and she went back inside and I just stood in that corner for a long time feeling like I would just prefer to die then to go to prison.

I mean this place was bad enough and some of the guys that were in real prisons were telling me about what it was like in a real prison and I was almost scared to death to go there.

I looked at the clock on the wall and I had been standing in that corner for a little over an hour at this point in time. I was still feeling sick but I did not throw up anymore.

My legs were shaking in fear and my feet were hurting from having to stand there in the corner for so long a time, especially in those five inch heels.

Another half hour went by when I saw a vehicle coming down the long driveway towards the house. My tummy started to do flips again and I was afraid that I was going to throw up again, but I guess there was nothing left in my stomach to come out. As the vehicle got closer it did not look like a prison van, but a car.

As the car got closer it looked like Cally's car, but then there are a lot of mustangs around. The car parked in the parking lot and Cally did get out of the car. As Cally walked towards the house she could see me standing in the corner being very unsteady on my five inch high heels.

Cally looked up at me with a face that I had never seen before. Cally did not say a word to me, rather Cally walked in a hurry around to the front of the house.

Cally came up on the porch and I wanted to turn around to see her, but I was way too ashamed to do so. Cally stomped across the wood deck porch to me and grabbed my shoulder and turned me around and slapped me across the face as hard as she could.

Cally started to yell at me too, I JUST CANNOT BELEIVE YOU, I CAN'T BELEIVE YOU MORT!!!!!!!!! Cally was obviously physically as well as emotionally upset with me like I had never seen from her before.

Cally, continued to yell at me, I AM SO UPSET WITH YOU MORT I DON'T KNOW WHAT TO SAY!!!!!!! Cally raised her hand again like she was going to hit me again, but took a deep breath and lowered her hand.

TURN AROUND MORT!!!!!! I CAN'T EVEN LOOK AT YOU!!!!!!!!!! Cally yelled at me. I turned around and Cally went inside the house. I just stood in that corner and started crying. I had never been that upset in my life. About 10 minutes later Cally came back out and told me to come with her and Cally took me into the guest office and slammed the door behind us.

Cally sat down behind the desk and had me stand in the middle of the room. Cally was not yelling anymore, she was more like just flat out upset with me. Cally told me that since this prison thing started that she has done everything she possible could to keep me out of a real prison and she was obviously successful.

But, NO!!!!!!!!!!!! that was not good enough for you, Mort. NO!!!!!!!!! you had to go an commit another crime. I AM JUST SO UPSET MORT, SO UPSET, I CANNOT THINK STRAIGHT!!!!!!!!!! Another 5 years in a real prison, that's 15 years Mort, 15 years, I would be old when you got out!

Mort, I came here today, and as angry with you as I am, I would have said or did anything to get you out of this new mess you got yourself into. Mort, I would have sucked that mans cock if I had to. I would have let him have sex with me if I had to.

I would have even let him fuck me in the ass if I had too.

Mort, I would give that man my virginity, if I still had it, for you. THAT'S HOW MUCH I LOVE YOU!!!!!

Cally pointed to a corner and told me to go and stand in that corner. Before I even got to the corner, Cally burst out in tears and just cried and cried and cried and cried some more. I think Cally cried longer and harder than I do when they beat me.

I felt so bad, so bad, that I could not possibly describe it too you. I would have done anything to make Cally feel better, I could not believe that I was standing here in this corner waiting to go to prison for 15 years and all I could think about was how I hurt Cally.

I could not believe that Cally told me that she loved me. As bad as I was feeling that made me feel so wonderful, a more wonderful feeling then I ever felt before. I loved Cally too!!!!!!

It was breaking my heart standing in that corner that day listening to Cally cry and cry and cry. About 15 minutes went by before Cally finally stopped crying. Turn around Mort, Cally said.

As I turned around to see Cally's ever so distressed face, she pointed to her face and said, Mort, you see this face? Yes Cally, I want you to look at this face and I want you to burn this face into your soul and I never, never, ever, want you to make this face show up again, DO YOU UNDERSTAND ME!!!!!!!!!!!!!!!!!!!!!!!!! MORT?

I was crushed and I even felt like that I deserved to go to prison, not for what I did to Sabrina or what I did to

Ally, or even bribing the Boss, but for what I did to Cally. I LOVED HER TOO!!!!!!!!!!

I was physically and emotionally crushed by the distress I saw on Cally face that day and I told myself that I would never cause Cally's beautiful face to look like that again. That day changed my life. Cally changed my life that day, when she told me she loved me.

BACK IN THE CORNER MORT!!!!!!!! I turned around again and faced the corner and Cally left the room and came back in about 5 minutes and told me to come with her. As I turned around I noticed that Cally had not washed her face and still had a tear stained, makeup dripped face.

As I followed Cally to the front porch I was feeling that I just hated myself for hurting Cally so much, I just felt worse than I ever thought I could possibly feel. I really did love Cally and I could not stand that feeling of hurting her.

The Boss was out on the porch waiting for us, Cally took me over to him and told the Boss, put him over the hitch and give him 100 with the long cane! The Boss got up and looked at Cally and asked her if she wanted to wash up and Cally told him NO! I want him to see the face he caused!

The Boss took me over to the wood hitch that unfortunately I was all too familiar with as I have been punished over the hitch already. The Boss tied me down in the usual four point position, but, even tighter than in the past. The Boss walked over to the porch and got the long cane, the cane that hurts the most.

Cally was sitting in one of the rocking chairs on the porch and Miss Anne brought her an ice tea. THWACK!!!!!!!!!! THWACK!!!!!!!!!!   THWACK!   THWACK!!!!!!!!!! THWACK!!!!!!!!!! THWACK!!!!!!!!!! THWACK !!!!!!!!!! THWACK!!!!!!!!!!!!! THWACK!!!!!!!!!! THWACK!!!!!!!! THWACK!!!!!!!!!!

The Boss was killing me with that cane that day and was crying after the first ten strokes. Although I thought I was crying sooner and harder as I was really crying about hurting Cally and not the increasing pain in my ass.

THWACK!!!!!!!!   THWACK!!!!!!!!   THWACK!!!!! THWACK!!!!!!!!!!   THWACK!!!!!!   THWACK!!!!! THWACK!!!!!! THWACK!!!!! THWACK!!!!! THWACK!!!!! THWACK!!! THWACK!!!!! THWACK!!!!! THWACK!!!! THWACK!!!! THWACK!!!! THWACK!!!!! THWACK!!!!! On and on and on and on, as I screamed and cried and screamed and cried some more.

The Boss was hitting me with full hard strokes, 20 strokes from my left side and then 20 strokes from my right side and back to the left and back to the right. All that could be heard for the next 10 minutes was THWACK!!!!!!!!!!!!!!! me screaming and me crying.

THWACK!!!!!!!   THWACK!!!!!!!!!!   THWACK!!!!!!!!!! THWACK!!!!!!!!!!! THWACK!!!!!!!!! Finally the Boss stopped caning me and looked over towards Cally and told her that was 80 Miss. Cally did not hesitate and told the Boss, that she said 100. But, Miss, the damage?

Cally got up and walked over to me and looked at my ass that was just one big huge mass of welts and told the Boss, 20 more. Cally stood there and got an up close view of my last 20 as I just could not scream or cry any harder as the Boss and that cane were punishing me so, so badly.

After I received the full 100 welts, the Boss told Cally 100 Miss. Cally told the Boss to give me another 50 on my thighs. I think that took all the rest of the very little energy I had left to accept this punishment and I just slumped and hung over the rail while the boss started anew on my legs.

Cally went back to the porch and sat down and I stayed there and the Boss, THWACK!!!!!!!! THWACK!!!!!!!!!! THWACK!!!!!!!!! THWACK!!!!!!!! THWACK!!!!!!!! THWACK!!!!!!!!!!!! THWACK!!!!!!!!!! THWACK!!!!!!!!!!!!

For another 5 minutes, as I just hung there and screamed and cried and cried and cried and cried!!!!!!!!!!!!! THWACK!!!!!!!!! THWACK!!!!!! THWACK!!!!!!!!!! THWACK!!!!!!!!!!! THWACK!!!!!!!! THWACK!!!!!!!!!!! on and on and on, THWACK!!!!!!!!!! THACK!!!!!!!!!! THWACK!!!!!!!!

Another 5 minutes of nothing but, THWACK!!!!!! THWACK!!!!!!!! THWACK!! THWACK!!!!!! THWACK!!!!! THWACK!!!!! THWACK!!!!! THWACK!!!!! THWACK!!! THWACK!!!!!!! Like with that extra severe strapping I got from the Boss that day, I thought that the Cane was whipping the skin right off me legs.

But that did not stop the THWACK!!!!!!!!!!!!!! THWACK!!!!!!!!!! THWACK!!!!!!! THWACK!!!!!! While I just screamed and cried and screamed and cried and screamed and cried some more. THWACK!!!!!!!

THWACK!!!!!   THWACK!!!!!!   THWACK!!!!!!!
THWACK!!!!!!!!

I was so distressed at this point that when the Boss stopped caning me I did not even noticed. The Boss untied me and helped me to my feet and hooked me wrist cuffs behind my back again and walked me back to the porch.

As I saw Cally still there in her chair, I could not look at her as I was just overwhelmed with shame for hurting her this way, Cally was the best thing that ever happened to me in my life so far and I would do anything for her.

As I went up the steps looking at the ground so I did not have to face Cally. Cally, barked at me, MORT, YOU LOOK AT ME! I raised my eyes to look at Cally and Cally said, MORT YOU SEE THIS FACE? THIS IS THE FACE THAT YOU CAUSED MORT!!!!!!!!!!!!!! BACK TO THE CORNER!!!!!!!!

Under normal circumstances I would have not had the strength to stand in the corner after a beating like that, but under these circumstance I needed to obey Cally as I disappointed her too much already and I somewhere found the strength to stand in the corner again so that I could obey Cally.

That was really a hellacious beating, but it was nothing more then I deserved for giving Cally "THAT FACE" I was so full of shame and disappointment in myself, it was making me feel sick again. I have embarrassed and humiliated Cally and I was having a real problem with that, how could I ever make it up to her?

Cally and the Boss went back inside the house and left me standing there in the corner with my own well earned tear stained face. Cally came back about 10 minutes later and told me to come with her. Cally had washed her face and looked much better.

Cally took me back into the office and showed me a piece of paper and told me to sign it!!!!!!!!!!!!!! I was going to read it, but I did not, I just obeyed Cally and signed it. If I had learned anything in life so far it was that I was better off if I just obey Cally, so I did.

Cally took the paper and made a copy for me and told me to post it on the wall in my room and to read it every morning before I left for work.

The paper said;

On this day, I tried to bribe the Boss into giving me better working conditions.

At no time did the Boss ask for such a bribe, or even indicated to me that he would be agreeable to discuss such a bribe.

The bribe was totally my idea and the Boss not only turned me down, but punished me severely for offering said bribe.

I understand that I have committed a crime and 5 years could be added to my sentence.

I further understand that if I complete my four years of prison camp without ever going to prison, that these charges of which I herein pled guilty to, will never be prosecuted.

Signed and dated by me.

Cally told me to follow her and we went back to the porch where the Boss was sitting. Cally told the Boss, here you can have him back now! I have had enough of him for one day, however Sir, Cally added, I want him to stand in the corner with his shorts around his ankles and his panties around his knees everyday for the next two weeks for 30 minutes during breakfast, lunch, and dinner! That's an hour and a half each and every day! Sure thing, Miss, the Boss said.

One more thing Sir, in two weeks I will be coming back here and I want you to give him a good long hard whipping in addition to today's punishment! Alright Miss, if that's want you want.

That's what I want Sir and I thank you in advance for your cooperation in this unfortunate matter. However, Sir, I don't think you will have any more problems with SISSY after today.

Cally then told me to get down on my knees and told the Boss to stand up. Cally and the Boss must have discussed this when I was not around as the Boss seemed to know what to do.

The Boss moved over and stood in front of me and then turned his back to me and dropped his pants to the floor and pushed his underwear down to his knees and bent over a little. The Boss reached back and used his hands to spread his ass cheeks a little.

Cally looked over to me and told me to give him the "Kiss". I knew what Cally wanted me to do and I had no choice but to do it. I would have done anything Cally told me to do that day, and in fact I did.

I then put my lips up to his ass hole and gave him a few soft kisses and then used my tongue to French kiss his ass hole as well and then removed my face from his ass crack and leaned back on my haunches hoping that was all I had to do. Cally barked at me, that's fine sissy get up! Now, Cally was calling me sissy for the first time.

The Boss pulled his underwear and pants back up and looked over to Cally and said that was interesting. Sir, that was extremely humiliating for sissy. It will help him learn to be more obedient.

Cally looked at me and barked at me that she would be back in two weeks and that God help me if I get into an more trouble between now and then. YOU UNDERSTAND ME, SISSY!!!!!!!!!!!!! ? Yes Cally.

As Cally started to walk away, I called to her? Cally turned back towards me, I am sorry Cally. Cally almost smiled and said, I KNOW! sissy, I know, but you will learn to obey me, it's just a matter of how much you need to be punished before we get there.

Then Cally pointed to the Boss, indicating that I also need to say I was sorry to him, I shook my head yes.

Cally walked quickly to her car and drove off. The Boss

looked at me and told me that he does not know where I found that lady, but that I should never let her go. The Boss said that Cally was the smartest person he has ever met, man or women, and God knows what she sees in you, sissy.

Sir? Yes sissy? I am sorry I tried to bribe you and thank you for punishing me for my mistake. Yea, the Boss said, I know you're sorry. Cally told me that you did not mean to insult me, that you just grew up thinking that you could buy anything you wanted and did not mean any disrespect to me. Cally told me that you are just not smart enough to have figured that out on your own.

Sissy, believe me! If Cally did not explained that to me, you would be on your way to the real prison right now instead of on your way back to the barn. You owe that young lady your life and from what I understand it's not the first time. No, Sir, it's not.

That night I posted that letter of agreement on my wall as Cally told me to, laid down in bed and thought about how much I had hurt Cally and how much I hated to see how much she looked hurt, and how much I realized that I loved her, and I cried myself to sleep.

As I was walking to the barn the next morning, I could feel that my life was different now. I felt like instead of me trying to be what I thought I should be, a man, or what I have been in life so far, I felt like my goal was to please Cally, nothing more and nothing less.

Cally was all I could think about, I wanted to make her proud of me now. It did not matter what I was told to do or how humiliating I found the task, or how embarrassed

I was. I would obey Cally and work to regain her trust. Cally owned me, my body and my soul. But, that did not feel like a bad thing to me, rather it felt like a good thing.

For the next two weeks I spent my hour and a half everyday, 7 days a week standing in the corner while all the guys looked at my welts that covered me from the very top of my ass to my knees. It was hard to find and white spots, just all angry red lines of swollen welts.

I was the best behaved over those two weeks since I came here. I worked and served and worked and served everyday and I seemed happier doing it and I was more friendly to the guys and I went out of my way to get them whatever they needed.

I think that they noticed my improved attitude as well, as they stopped teasing me and touching me and asking for blow jobs, etc. I spent all that time standing in the corner and all I could think about was how I wanted to make Cally happy and I accepted my corner time as no less then I deserved for upsetting Cally.

So now you know why this was the worst day of my life, it was not the beating, it was not the thoughts of going to prison, it was Cally's face, "THIS FACE" as Cally called it.

That was the worst moment of my life and I never wanted to do anything to ever make Cally have "THAT FACE" again. Cally deserves better and I was committed to see that she got better, especially from me.

That was the best day I my life, because Cally told me that she loved me, my life changed forever that day.

MORE NEW CLOTHES:

Two days later, December 3rd, to add to my punishment Pete brought me some more new clothes and told me to get dressed.

My new top was basically the same, as short midriff top the ended just below my chest area. However, it was much bigger than the ones I had been wearing and I was confused as the one I had on fit rather well.

Then I looked in the next box and I found a bra and some false breast inserts. After putting on the bra and the falsies, I could see why the top needed to be larger to accommodate my new bigger chest.

There was a box with a couple of wigs inside and I put one on and it was short, shoulder length, but real full and made my head look very feminine.

Then there was a box with several skirts inside. They were all real short, like tennis shirts, all pleaded in different colors.

Last, the was some makeup in a bag.

Just as I was finished getting dressed, Miss Anne came by and put some of that red makeup on my cheeks and showed me how to rub in so my face had a rosy color to it.

Then Miss Anne showed me how to put the glossy lip stick on to make my lips look very kissable, she said.

Last, Miss Anne gave me a few razors and some shaving cream and told me that from now on I need to keep my legs shaved as well as my face. Shaving was not a big problem for me as I had very little and very light facial hair.

My legs were the same way, very light peach fuzz type of hair that is easily shaved and easily kept clean.

There was a note from Cally. Sissy, I am still furious with you. Here are your new clothes that you are to wear every day. When you stand in the corner for me in the barn, you are to stand there like you use to make me stand in the corner with your panties around your knees, your hands bound behind your back with wrist cuffs while you hold up the back of your skirt to show off your punished ass!

SISSY, DON'T DISAPPOINT ME AGAIN!!!!!!!!!!!!!!!!!!!!!! !!!!!!!!!!!!!!

As you could imagine, I was a big hit with all the other guys. Now, I really looked like a girl and a funny thing happened. The other guys did not tease me as much and actually treated me with more respect as if I was really a girl. Strange I thought, but fine with me.

When I was standing in the corner three times a day, I felt much more humiliated dressed like that as I was holding up the back of my skirt.

The other strange thing that happened, was that I looked

at myself in the mirror and I liked what I saw. I did look like a sexy young girl and I felt like a sexy young girl and I liked the way that looked and felt.

What was wrong with me ???????????

It was December 15th, as you can imagine, I always look forward to seeing Cally, after all, Cally is the high light of my life at that point, the only good part of my life.

However, by seeing Cally that time, I also knew that I was going to get another whipping and I just hated to scream and cry in front of Cally the way I do.

Of course, I did not want another whipping either, but I had nothing to say about that, it was up to Cally. In fact, everything seemed to be up to Cally anymore, even what happened to me there at the Reform Farm.

Nevertheless, I had a degree of bittersweet excitement as I looked forward to seeing Cally this day. Cally usually gets there early and waits for my on the porch deck. However, as I walked towards the house that day I did not see Cally, maybe she was inside I thought. Although the Boss was sitting on the porch where Cally usually sits.

As soon as the Boss saw me he got up and walked down the porch steeps and told me to strip, yes Boss. I took off all my clothes, except my lace socks and five inch high heels.

The Boss put the wrist cuffs on me and strung me up to the yard arm to whip me. However, the Boss told me that Cally will be a little late, that I was to wait for her there, as the Boss laughed as he knew that I was not going anywhere.

I could see the driveway from where I was bound with my hands tied together way up over my head to the point where I could just reach the ground with the toes of my high heels.

About 10 minutes later I saw Cally's car coming up the to the parking lot. Cally got out of the car and in spite of my position and my absolute fear of another whipping I managed a smile for Cally. Cally had something in her hand as she got closer to me I could see that it was a whip.

Cally walked up to my face and she still looked angry with me, very angry! Cally told me that she is still furious with me for thinking that I was so damn smart that I could bribe the Boss. 15 YEARS YOU COULD HAVE GOT, SISSY 15 YEARS!!!!!!!!!!

You see this whip, sissy, this whip is going to give you the whipping of your life and I am going to whip you myself with it. Sissy, when I am finished with you today, you will never disobey me again, NEVER!

Cally's uncoiled the whip before my eyes. Cally's whip was longer then the Bosses, maybe 16 feet long, but very thin. I still assumed that Cally could not be all that good with a whip as she had no experience so I figured that I was lucky that Cally was going to whip me. However, I had underestimated Cally in the past and she has always surprised me, today would be no different.

Cally and her whip and walked around behind me and

I heard a tremendous SNAP!!!! That SNAPING sound was immediately followed by the pain on my back that I could not describe that it hurt so much. SNAP!!!! I grunted, SNAP!!!!!! I grunted in pain, SNAP!!!!!! AHHH!!!!! SNAP!!!!!! OUCH!!!!!!!!! SNAP!!!! AHHHH !!!!!! SNAP!!!! OUCH!!!!!

WOW!!!!!!!!! I could not believe how much this whipping was hurting me. That was only five or six lashes and I was yelling OHCH!!!!! OUCH!!!!! OUCH!!!!!!! OUCH!!!!!!!!!!!!! after each lash. I could not believe that Cally could whip me so hard or should I say so well.

Cally's lashes actually hurt more than the Bosses. SNAP!!!!!!!!! And I started crying already. SNAP!!!!!!!!!!! SNAP!!!!!!!!! OUCH!!!!!!! OUCH!!!!!!! OUCH!!!!!!! The Boss's whipping hurt more like a hard strike that was deep down, more like a punch.

However, Cally's whipping feel much more like a thousand bees stinging and gave more of a hot bite to my back, SNAP!!!!!!!!! SNAP!!!!!!!!!! SNAP!!!!!! AHH!!!!!! OUCH!!!!!! I tried to run away, but my legs were not going anywhere, it was just a natural reaction to the tremendous pain.

That's about 15 lashes and I was already crying in earnest. Cally was whipping me so hard, so hard, OUCH!!!!!!!!! AHHH!!!!!! hard. I could not know how Cally learned to whip me so well? SNAP!!!!!!! SNAP!!!!!!!!!! SNAP!!!!!!!!!! SNAP!!!!!!!

I burst into uncontrollable tears as I struggled with all my strength to move away from the lashes, but I knew I was going nowhere tied up like this. AHHH!!!!

I screamed after each lash as I gasp for breath thru my mouth as my nose was already clogged with snot. So, so much PAIN!!!!!

There was really nothing to think about other then how long will this whipping last. Over my own screaming and crying I could hear nothing other than SNAP!!!!!!!!!!!! SNAP!!!!!!!!!!!! SNAP!!!!!!!!!!!! SNAP!!!! As Cally continued to whip me and whip me hard, how did she learn to do this I wondered?

If Cally wanted me to know that she was fully capable of punishing me than she has made her point. That was the hardest whipping to take. If Cally wanted me to know how angry she was with me, then she has explained it and explained it loud and clear.

The whipping stopped after about 40 or 50 lashes as apparently Cally moved her position. Then all I heard was a whistle and OUCH!!!!!!!!! OUCH!!!!!! OUCH!!!!! OUCH!!!!! OUCH!!!!!!! I was rocked with more pain and more pain and more pain.

I have never felt anything like it before. SNAP!!!!!!!!!! SNAP!!!!!!!!! SNAP!!!!!!!!!! SNAP!!!!!!!!!!!! SNAP!!!!!!!!! The pain from Cally's whip was actually worse than the pain from the punishment cane.

The whipping continued about one lash every 10 seconds or so, numbering 60, 70 through 80 or more. Cally worked the whip down the rest of my back towards my waist but did not actually whipped my waist line. I assumed that Cally knew the whip may not be good for the kidney area and that's why Cally did not whip any lower.

I was sure that my back looked just like a ladder, and with SNAP!!!!! SNAP!!!!!!!! SNAP!!!!!!!!!! SNAP!!!!!! SNAP!!!!! I was just one big mess of snot, tears, screaming, and being as sorry as I could have been then I disappointed Cally.

In fact, the pain in my heart for disappointing Cally was actually worse than the whipping on my back. I never wanted to feel such hurt in my heart again, never.

OUCH!!!!!!!!!!!!!!! I screamed the loudest with that lash as I was having more trouble breathing at this point as my nose was totally clogged with snot from all the crying, so I had to scream and then cry and then try to breath in between.

Cally stopped whipping me again and I was hoping she was finished as I surely learned my lesson and was ready to obey Cally's every command. But, more so and more importantly I never wanted to disappoint Cally again.

Cally, apparently was not finished teaching me my lesson as she just moved around to my other side and then SNAP!!!!!!!!! SNAP!!!!!!!!! SNAP!!!!!! SNAP!!!!!!!! SNAP!!!!!!!!!! Lash number 90 or 100 or 110 maybe struck home and I screamed the loudest and the longest and I just slumped in place with my bounds then holding me up by my wrists, as my toes were just sort of hanging there.

Cally started anew at the top of my back and WOW another SNAP!!!!!! SNAP!!!!!!!!!! SNAP!!!!!!!!!! SNAP!!!!!!!!!! SNAP!!! SNAP!!!!!!!!!!!! That last lash wrapped around to my chest and gave me the same electric shock to my left nipple that my right one experienced earlier and I thought that I was bleeding a bit.

This whipping was far longer than the whippings I got at the Reform farm so far and Cally did not seem to be losing any steam as Cally just kept whipping me and whipping me and whipping me. SNAP!!!!!!! SNAP!!!!!!! SNAP!!!!!!!! SNAP!!!!!!!!!!! SNAP!!!!!! seemly as hard as Cally could whip me.

I must have received about 100 to 125 lashes so far and now Cally was whipping over areas that already have big fat painful welts on them and SNAP!!!!!! SNAP!!!!!!!!!!! SNAP!!!!!!! SNAP!!!!!!!!!! SNAP!!!!!!

That was making the pain even worse, which was hard for me to believe that any lash could hurt more than the previous lashes, but damn if they didn't.

So far that whipping had lasted for probably 20 minutes at a lash rate of 6 lashes per minute. MAN! That was a long time to be whipped by anybody and a really long time for a whipping this bad. All I could do was moan, cry, and scream some more. I guess one does not run out of tears and they just keep pouring out of my eyes.

I was hurting so much that I did not have much struggle left in me. I was having more and more trouble keeping at least one of my toes on the ground to give my arms help in holding myself up as I was still swinging a bit as I struggled to receive each new lash.

Cally stopped whipping me for a minute while she changed sides again. This time Cally started to whip me again but totally different, not across my back from top to bottom anymore this time.

Cally used no pattern as before this time not as much time in between lashes giving me no time to recover as the pace was only about 5 seconds or less between lashes.

SNAP!!!!!!!!!!!!! SNAP!!!!!!!!!!!!! SNAP!!!!!!!!!!! SNAP!!!!!!!!! SNAP!!!!!!!!!! SNAP!!!!!!!!! SNAP!!!!!!!!!!!!! SNAP!!!!!!!! SNAP!!!! SNAP!!!!!!!!!!!!! AS Cally continued to punish me like I have never been punished before. Cally also seemed to allow only the last 12 to 15 inches of the whip to strike me then instead of maybe 20 to 25 inches as before.

This pattern provided even a louder SNAP!!!!!!!!!!!!!!! as the closer to the end of a whip you get the faster the whip is traveling and therefore it makes more sound and strikes even harder. This pattern also provides a bigger sting but not as much deep down pain as before.

However, as Cally was whipping me all over my back, she continues whipping over the welts that were already there making them hurt even worse. Add that to the increased rhythm, the pain was so bad that I thought that I may pass out. I actually wished I did.

Those more painful lashes were given at full speed and landed anywhere Cally wanted, one across, one up and down as opposed to across so that it would crisis crossed the other welts. Having, four, five , six, seven, eight, nine, and ten, the whipping continued and continued and continued which 12 lashes every minute now.

I was basically just hanging by my wrists at that point as I had no strength left in my legs and this hanging position was making it even more difficult for me to breath and continue to cry my eyes out. I did not even seem to have the strength to scream as much anymore but did more groaning. The crying continued with tears all over the place and snot dripping and flying out of my nose.

Two minutes or so later Cally was up to about 150 or maybe 175 lashes and the whipping stopped. I was just hanging there by my wrist cuffs with no strength to do anything but cry. My back hurt like nothing that I could ever imagine.

Cally left me there to hang by my wrists and to cry and cry and whimper some more. Cally left me hanging there for about 15 minutes more until I stopped crying, but I was still having trouble breathing and finding the energy to stand on my toes again to take the pressure off my arms. I struggled to do so however as my arms were getting real sore.

During that 15 minute time frame I could hear Cally and the Boss on the porch talking, but I could not hear well enough to make out what they were saying. I think I was crying to loud to hear anything, as they were not that far away from me.

Cally came back and stood in front of me with the whip coiled up in her hand. Cally shook the whip at me and scolded me very loudly that next time I have any ideas about anything other than to obey, or obey, obey, or obey some more, that I need to get permission from her first.

Sissy, you hear me? Yes Cally. Yes sissy, but did you understand me? You either obey or you asked me permission, there are no other choices for you. GOT IT, SISSY?

Good sissy. Two more things sissy. I am still angry with you sissy. After all, you were a phone call away from going to prison for 15 years. So, sissy, I will not be coming back until I feel better. I do not know how long that may be?

Number two sissy! When I do come back I better find the most well behaved sissy that either of us has ever known, You better be so obedient so that I do not find even one bruise on your body from another punishment. YOU HEAR ME SISSY?????????? Yes Cally.

Cally started to walk away, but stopped herself and turned back towards me. Sissy, I do love you so very much, that's why I am so upset with you. I tried to smile but my mouth did not seem to be working.

Nevertheless, Sissy, in addition to this whipping, you are to spend an additionally two weeks standing in the corner for breakfast, lunch, and dinner, do you hear me Sissy? Yes Cally. Cally turned and walked away.

A few minutes later the Boss and Rick came and helped me down and helped me back to my room. The Boss told me that I could stay there until I had the strength to come out. Thank you, Boss.

Several times over the next week while I was standing in the corner with my back aching from that whipping, I could hear some of the guys taking about Cally.

In addition to the regular chatter about how beautiful Cally was and how lucky a clown I have to be to have a girl like that pay any attention to me. It seemed to be the majority opinion of the whole group, including Rick and Pete and the Boss, that Cally was much more punishing then the Boss. They also thought that Cally expects even more perfect obedience then the Boss does.

Some of the guys thought that was a bad thing and wondered why I put up with Cally. While others thought that if they had a girl like Cally that she would keep them out of trouble.

In spite of that whipping Cally gave me and my additional two more weeks of standing in the corner, I believed that I was lucky to have a lady like Cally and that loved me enough to punish me and try to keep me out of trouble.

CALLY VISITS AFTER CHRISTMAS:

On December 27th, I was told that Cally was coming to see me that day at 2 pm. I was so excited to see Cally that day and I was even more excited to be able to tell her that I obeyed her and stayed out of trouble. Pete told me that Cally would be here at the regular time of 2 pm so that I could finish cleaning up after lunch before see her.

As I walked up to the house Cally was on the front porch waiting for me. I walked up the steps and stood next to Cally waiting to see how she would treat me after last time. Cally told me to turn around and lower my panties.

Cally lifted up the back of my skirt to check out my ass cheeks. Lucky for me that Cally did not find any punishment marks. So far the reception was real cold, but I was not going to say anything even though I wanted to grab Cally and kiss her and hug her and fuck her right there on the porch.

If Cally had me turn around she would have found a hard cock in her face. Cally had me pull my panties back up and told me to come inside with her and we went into the office.

Sissy, I love the new clothes, you are looking more and more like a the sexy girlfriend that I was hoping for. You even have learned to walk very well with a nice wiggle. With the wig and the makeup, I think you could pass on the street for a real girl. UMMMM, my pussy likes!!!!!

However, today, I am still angry with you so business first Cally said in a cold tone, not even a smile. Cally showed me pictures of the new house and I was surprised how fast it was getting built. Cally told me that she meets with the contractor every week and they were two weeks ahead of schedule.

Cally showed me my Brokerage statement that just came in yesterday and I looked at it and told Cally that there seems to be even more money in there then I would have thought again.

Cally, in a real calm tone, said OH YES! I took another $10,000.00 of you money and bought another option on oil and made an extra $90,000.00 over the past six weeks.

$90,000.00 this time Cally? So, Cally, you made an extra $355,000.00 in under six months since I gave you control of my account? That's right, sissy, I have made you $355,000.00 and kept you out of prison twice in the last 6 months.

So, SISSY, what have you done for me except disobey me? I just looked at Cally, what could I say, she was 100% correct. Cally was wonderful to me and I was nothing but trouble to her.

Cally, there is no way I could be any more sorry for all the trouble I have caused you and I could not appreciate all the wonderful things you have done for any more. I will do my very best to be the most obedient and loving "girl" friend I can be to you from now on and forever, Cally, I love you to no end. I almost got a smile from Cally at that point, but she changed the subject.

Cally, we talk about all sorts of things when you came and visit, but we never talk about money. Would you like some money for anything? Cally smiled and laughed a little.

Sissy, I have access to your six million dollars, if I wanted some money I would have taken it. So, no, sissy, I don't need any money. However, it was kind of you to be concerned about me and ask. Cally's tone was still not a happy one.

Sissy, I only have two goals in life right now, the second is getting good marks in college and the First and most important is getting you back home to me as soon as I can.

Cally, yes sissy? Truthfully, what kind of future do you expect for us. You can't change the fact that you are a lesbian? Cally again laughed at me and told me, don't be silly sissy, of course I cannot stop being a lesbian. So, I am going to turn you into my girlfriend and that way we can both be happy.

I just looked at Cally and said nothing. Cally is always saying things like that to me and I never understand them, so why should this time be any different?

After all, Cally still thinks that I am going to be her sissy maid some day. I mean, how silly is that thought? But,

I guess I will just let her dream as it seems to make her happy.

Alright Cally said, enough of the business, let's chat about you. Sissy, I see that you been a good boy for me since we last met? Yes, Cally. I told Cally how well I have behaved and how much nicer and helpful I have been to the other guys and how I took my corner time with the proper attitude. Even though it was an hour and a half a day for four straight weeks of skirt up, panties down corner time.

Excellent Cally said, this time with her nice big smile. Alright then sissy, stand up. I stood up and Cally got down on her knees in front of me and reached up under my skirt and lowered my panties. Cally told me to tuck the front of my skirt into the elastic band and Cally then saw a rock hard cock staring her in the face.

Cally looked up to me and licked her lips and opened her mouth and sucked my cock all the way into her mouth like it was something she did everyday and it was second nature to her.

Cally bobbed her head up and down my shaft only a few times and I came in her mouth. Cally acted all excited to receive my cum and gobbled it up like she was extra hungry. Cally kept my cock in her mouth as she sucked all the cum off of it and the slowly let it out.

Cally stood up and said, see sissy, is it not better to be a good girl? After all, is that not what you taught me, sissy? Yes Cally. What else was there to say, except, thank you Cally.

Alright Cally said, sissy I want you to tell me what you think and what you felt about last time I was here. I took a deep breath and told Cally that the short version was that I made a huge mistake, that she saved me, again! That I was punished severely for it and I deserved my punishment.

And, the long version Cally asked? Well, the long version was that every time you come here I am surprised that you even bother to come. I am surprised by something you tell me every single time. I am more thankful then I could ever tell you that you saved me from prison, for the second time.

I was absolutely crushed that I upset you so much and I promise you today that I will never cause you to have "THAT FACE" again, ever! I was happier then I have ever been in my whole life to hear that you loved me, even though I have no idea why. I was thrilled to tell you that I love you too, which I surly do!

You were more than correct to have me punished so harshly and I can only hope that my great suffering that day made you feel better even if just a little. I have been a Bad Boy many times in my life and with your continued help, perhaps I can live up to my father's wishes and be a good boy, or girl for you. However, Cally, I have already proved that I did not do it for him, I want so badly to do it for you, Cally.

I want to be a good girl for you Cally, only for you! I want to give you a reason to love me Cally. I want to give you a reason to believe in me, Cally. I want to make you happy, Cally. I want to earn your respect and make you proud me, Cally, I cannot gift you with those things, they need to be earned and I intend to earn them from you.

Cally started to cry and so did I a little. We sat on the couch for maybe 15 minutes and hugged and cuddled and said nothing.

I did not ask Cally how she felt about that day, I thought she made herself clear enough with "THAT FACE".

We spoke about many things for the rest of the afternoon, so long in fact, that I was late in getting back to the barn for setting up for dinner.

On the way out, we passed the Boss who was sitting on the front porch and Cally told him that she was sorry about keeping me so long. The Boss looked at Cally and told her it was no problem that she was welcome to stay as long as she wished, anytime.

I walked Cally to the car. Cally looked at me and said tell me, sissy! I smiled at Cally and told her that I promise that I will try my very best to be completely obedient until see her again. Cally gave me real nice hug and a great long kiss with plenty of tongue for the first time in a while.

One more thing before I leave, sissy. I am happy with how things have gone for the past month, but I am still not past "THAT FACE" you gave me, I am still angry with you.

So, I wanted to let you know that I have arranged a special punishment for you with all the girls here as they would be coming for you six month punishment anyway. So, I wish to punish you one more time and entertain them at the same time.

As with most of your punishments, sissy, you will not like it, but I think it may ease my mind enough for me to get past that last TRICK of yours. However, sissy, if you are missing my point here, it is that the girls think that they are coming to see you get punished for their pleasure only.

But, the truth is, you are going to be punished for me again as I am still angry with you and I need to get over it. But, only you and I need to know that part, sissy.

While I was walking back to the barn for dinner, I was thinking about that one comment that the one guy made about Cally being more strict and more punishing then the Boss.

Cally sure whipped me harder than the Boss did and Cally whipped me for a lot longer. Cally made me stand in the corner with my bare ass on display for 30 days times an hour and a half each and every day.

I mean Cally made me stand in the corner for 45 hours and had me caned by the Boss and then Cally whipped me herself all for the one problem. Although, I had to admit, it was sure a big problem.

However, I wondered how much of that was because I upset Cally compared to how much Cally needed to show the boss that I was properly punished.

I thought it was about 75% Cally and only 25% for the

Boss. So, I sure did agree with that guys opinion that Cally was much tougher then the Boss.

Nevertheless, I had no complaints about Cally, I loved her to no end and felt more sorry for upsetting her then upsetting the Boss. And, I guess I need someone strong like Cally to keep me out of trouble. I could not appreciate Cally anymore in spite of those severe punishments!

SIX MONTH VISIT BY THE GIRLS:

The Boss told me that everyone would come on January 3rd for my six month punishment. The morning of January 3rd I was really nervous and I had trouble sleeping the night before, as you could imagine.

I was about as nervous as I could be all morning while serving breakfast and then serving lunch. Pete came to me just after the guys went back to work after lunch and told me that the Boss wanted to see at the house at the usual time of 2 pm. However, sissy, before you go put on your wrist cuffs and ankle cuffs, yes Sir.

My tummy started to make those nervous jumping movements and I knew it was time for another humiliation session and another beating so that Sabrina and Ally could feel better about how I treated them. I put on the wrist and ankle cuffs and walked to the house.

It took a lot longer to walk to the house these days wearing these five inch high heels as I could only take small steps, but whatever, it is what it was.

However, I was beginning to really like my short skirts. I loved how they felt as I walked along and the bottom of the skirt would swish along under my ass cheeks and hit the back of my legs.

I enjoyed the breeze as it would flow up under the skirt and cool my panties. I especially enjoyed looking at myself in the mirror and thinking that I would fuck me. I think I have become a real dick teaser for a lot of these guys. They look at me a lot different than when I was Mort and just wore panties.

So, why do I feel sad about wearing these clothes. I thought it was just my internal feelings about what is expected of me as a man and I was not being manly at all. Nevertheless, I liked the clothes, especially the high heels, so I guess in a way I was internally fighting myself over what I actually liked and what I thought I should be.

As I got closer to the house I was thinking that it would be the first time the girls will get to see me in my complete set of nice girly clothes. Oh! what fun I thought as I started to get embarrassed in advanced.

As I got close enough to the porch where everyone could clearly see me, I only saw Ally, Sabrina, Steve, and Cally. Mindy and Molly I guess decided that they did not need to see me get punished any more. I was at least happy about that.

However, I also saw the two camera men that were getting good coverage of me as I walked down the driveway towards them. I guess everyone from school will be having a good time tonight seeing me dressed this way. Then I thought that maybe, just maybe they will not know it was me dressed this way with makeup and a wig?

Nevertheless, they filmed my entire punishment just

like last time and made sure they spent plenty of time filming me crying so everyone could see what a big sissy I really was and how much I was really being punished.

As I walked towards the steps, I was feeling even more embarrassed and to make things worse, I was getting an erection for my embarrassment. That was not helpful I thought, but then my cock had a mind of its own and I had nothing to say about it.

Cally stood up as I got to the stairs and smiled and asked everyone, with much enthusiasm in her voice, so how do you think Mort looks as a girl? They all started clapping in approval. I felt like hiding under a rock. My cock was enjoying itself, how strange I thought.

Cally made me come up on the porch to model for everyone, GREAT! As I stood there in front of Ally and Sabrina and Steve. I did not think that I could have been more embarrassed. Cally told me to turn around so they could see me from the back and that sure did not help.

Ally told Cally that she was right, that I do make a nice looking girlfriend and that I especially have nice sexy legs and a real nice ass holding out the back of my skirt.

I heard a horse and looked up around and saw Rick riding up on his horse. Then I noticed that Rick had something behind his horse that looked like one of those road barrier horses.

I did not have much time to pay attention as Cally moved over and stood in front of me. Cally whispered so the others could not hear her and reminded me that this was her punishing me, STILL, as a result of "THAT FACE" I caused.

Sissy, when we are finished here today, I don't think you will ever wish to disobey or disappoint me again. But, when we are finished, you let me know for sure. I just looked at Cally, still half ashamed by giving Cally "THAT FACE" and half scared as to how bad my punishment will be?

Cally, told me to take off all my clothes, everything, Cally said. I never thought that I would have wanted to keep my girly clothes on so badly. But, I actually preferred them over being naked in front a group of people who were all fully clothed.

Of course, I did as Cally told me to do and as I was removing my clothes the two camera men made sure they got good film of me before and as I stripped and then after when I was naked, except for the makeup. I guess there would no question about who I was then. And, now, everyone would know that I dress like a girl as well.

I was looking at what Rick had behind his horse. It was made out of wood and was in the shape of a horse, but without a horse head. The center piece was a landscaping timber which was an four foot long 2 inches across the top and 3 inches thick.

The landscaping timber was held up by two legs in the front and two legs in the back, all which had small air filled wheels attached to them. Then under the middle of the main landscaping timber was a cross bar where stirrups would have been if it was a real horse with a saddle.

Rick told me to come down once I was naked and told me to step up to the horse on the left side of the horse and swing one leg over the main landscaping timer. Once in place, I was actually sitting on the top of the main landscape timer, just like you would sit on a horse, only without a saddle.

But, keep in mind that this main timber was only about 2 inches wide and so I was actually sitting on that narrow 2 inch timber. This did not feel good and maybe that was the idea. No, I was sure that was the idea.

Too make things worse, Rick then hooked my ankle cuffs to hooks that was installed on that cross bar I told you about that was taking the place of the stirrups. Then Rick tightened the strap that held my ankle cuffs to the hooks so my legs were then pulled real tight so that I could not fall off this punishment horse. Rick then hooked my wrist cuffs behind my back.

This wood horse reminded me of was something I saw on the internet one time when I was shopping for discipline equipment when I bought the whips and the canes and the strap and the cuffs, etc. I think it was called a Chinese torture devise or something like that.

Only the one I saw on the internet had a pointed bar in the center, not a flat two inch bar like this one and they used it to make girls sit on it so that the pointed part would sit inside the girls pussy lips and all her weight would be pushing her pussy down on this pointed bar. That actually seemed even worse than this bar.

After I was "so called" mounted on this punishment horse, Rick got back on his horse pulled me along behind him while I was sitting on the two inch wide bar. Rick took me back to the barn as I bounced along sitting on that 2 inch bar and let me tell you, it did not feel good, not even a little bit.

I almost was bouncing up and down on the bar, but Rick had my legs secured pretty tight and that held me down and in place while the wood horse was bouncing along being pulled by Rick's horse.

I was thinking that it was actually better when I was being pulled by the horse when I was on foot and I had to keep up. This way that bar that I was sitting on that ran between my legs was just becoming more and more painful as I bounced along on top of it.

Rick pulled me and my punishment horse to the barn. The girls and Steve followed us to the barn so they got a good look at this newest form of punishment as I was humiliated as I could be about it, but what could I do.

The humiliation was not worth going to prison to avoid. Besides, as humiliated as I was, I knew that when my four years was up I would never need to see either of those bitches or Steve again and then my humiliation would be over for good. It's nice to have goals, right?

Rick got off his horse and unhooked my horse and rolled me half way in the barn door so that my back was facing the outside and I was facing the inside of the barn and I was directly below the center of the barn door frame. I noticed that all the guys were in the barn waiting for me to also enjoy my punishment. Great, just great, I thought.

This apparently was important as Rick came around behind me and unhooked my wrist cuffs and I was expecting Rick to unhook my feet to and let me up as I figured I was punished enough just being pulled around the farm on that two inch bar between my legs supporting all of my weight.

However, I should have known better as Rick pushed a button and a rope with another hook attached to it came down from the center of the barn door frame high above me. Rick attached that hook to my wrist cuffs in front of me and pushed the button again and it pulled my arms high up about my head until my arms were held very tight above my head. This did not take any pressure off my "sitting" area of my body that was still straddling that two inch timber and hurting me all the more.

Once I was in position Rick went over to the wall and picked up a strap and a whip that were hanging on the wall. Rick brought a strap and a whip over to me and laid them over the front of the horse where I could see them if I looked down. Rick then said to me, wait until you see what's going to happen today, it will be so much fun, as Rick gave me a big smile.

I looked at the strap and saw that it was not as wide or as thick as the one that was used to give my ass a strapping, rather it was about 2 inches wide and about four feet long and about 1/4 inch thick and it had a handle. The long length would indicate to me that it could be used the same as one would use a whip, to provide long high speed lashes.

Since I was sitting on this punishment horse, only my back is accessible, so who I thought was going to be having fun, certainly not me. The whip was about 12 feet long and looked just like the one that the Boss whipped the daylights out of me before.

Once I was in position, all three of the girls and Steve walked past me and took seats in the back of the barn at the last table. I would have expected those guys to say things or holler to the girls as you know how crude guys are.

But, They must have been warned to be perfectly respectable or else, as they were absolutely quiet and did not even look at the girls. I was impressed as Cally, Ally, and even Sabrina are all great looking young ladies.

Although Ally did dress like a slob with her torn jeans and T shirt. But, hell, she was still a nice looking girl in front of a bunch of guys who were female starved.

I kept closing my eyes as otherwise I had to look at all of those guys and the girls looking at me. But, Rick told me to keep my eyes open, so I guess I will have to see them seeing me, how embarrassing I thought. This just gets better and better all the time.

After Rick finished securing me with the rope, Rick went back in to the barn and picked up two jars. Rick told everyone that he had two jars with him. In the first jar had slips of paper with the names of each guy on them. In the second jar, there were slips of paper with numbers on them.

Risk was going to pick out three pieces of paper, one at a time, to choose the guys name. The chosen guy will then pick from the jar of numbers. When you matched the guy name with the number, that guy would get to whip me or strap me per the number of times on the second piece of paper.

After all the guys had a turn, the guy who beats me the hardest, as per a vote of all the other guys, gets a reward, I almost was thinking about how embarrassing this was, but all I could really think about is how much I was hurting sitting over this two inch wood timber, I was getting so sore.

Rick picked out the first name, George, and George went up to Rick and picked a number out of the second jar, the number was 15. George walked over to the front of the horse and picked up the whip, looked at me and said, this is really going to hurt sissy! Yes, I was scared, damn right I was scared, I was even starting to shake a little more in my legs.

George was a white guy that was thin and about 6 foot tall and did not have very big muscles. I was not sure why he was at the camp, but someone mentioned that he use to take drugs, so I assumed that his crime was drug related.

George did not keep me waiting very long when WHACK! The whip hit me from one side of my back to the other with the tip of the whip wrapping a bit around to my side. WHACK! WOW!, WOW! That hurt, it almost took my breath away. WHACK! I screamed, WHACK! AAHHH!!! WHACK!

After only five licks I burst into tears. I really wished that I could hold off the crying in front of Sabrina and Ally, but I knew that was not going to happen. I just found it so much more humiliating crying like a little girl in front of them.

WHACK! WHACK! WHACK! WHACK! WHACK! I screamed after each lash. I could do nothing else but cry and scream and cry and scream some more, it just hurt so much. The more I wiggled on this timber that I was sitting on the more I hurt in my ass and thigh area that were sitting on that wood bar. My nose again filled with snot and was dripping down my chin and onto my chest.

WHACK! WHACK! WHACK! WHACK! WHACK! That whip hurt so much I could not believe it. George finished his 15 lashes and Sabrina and Ally stood up and gave him a big hand. I guess the girls came to see me get punished again and again they are having a good time as Rick seems to really know how to punish me. You may remember that Rick hates me because I he heard me say that Rick was just a fucking nigger that enjoyed hurting white guys.

George put the whip back down in front of me, smiled at me and said that was real fun, you big cry baby. George went back and sat down. I just sat there still crying in front of all the guys that already thought that I was a sissy for crying when I was punished the other times.

I did not know how any of those guys could take a

whipping like this and not cry, but I guess that was just me as I have seen some of the other guys get punished and they grit their teeth and yell some and two of them did scream, but no tears, just tears from me, maybe I am a big sissy after all.

I stopped crying about 2 minutes later and Rick was already picking another name from his hat. Jose was chosen, now Jose was a gang member and had tattoos all over his arms and back and a couple on his chest. However it was his size that bothered me.

Jose was not that tall, maybe only 5 foot 9 inches tall, but he was built like a linebacker and had a big strong looking chest and big muscles in his arms and looked twice a strong as was George. Jose pulled the number 24 out of the other jar, meaning he was going to get to hit me 24 times with that whip.

Jose walked towards me and picked up the whip. Jose looked at me and said something in Spanish that I did not understand and then he laughed at me. Jose walked around behind me. However, Jose was left handed so he went to my right rear instead of my left.

WHACK! WHACK! WHACK! WHACK! WHACK! WOW!, OUW! WOW! OUCH! SCREAMING!!!!!! I could not take this whipping without crying as I burst into tears again and thought that I would not survive another 20 WHACK! WHACK! WHACK! from Jose as I could tell the difference from Jose who had a lot more force behind his WHACK! WHACK! WHACK! then did George. I wish I could pass out from the pain, but I did not, and I cried and yelled and WHACK! WHACK! WHACK! WHACK! WHACK! screamed !!!!!!!!!!!!!!!!!!!!

I was in so much pain I was losing my strength to even struggle against my bonds and started to just hung there being held on the horse with just my tightly bound legs that were holding in place on my wood horse.

WHACK! WHACK! WHACK! WHACK! WHACK! I SCREAMED!!!!! and SCREAMED !!!!!!!! and cried and almost chocked trying to breath and scream and cry all at the same time.

WHACK! WHACK! WHACK! WHACK! And Jose stopped and put the whip down again in front of me. Jose looked at me and said something else in Spanish but I could not really hear him over my own crying and moaning and yelling in pain, not only from the whip, but from the horse as well.

As Jose went back into the barn Sabrina and Ally got up again and gave him a big round of applause and Ally even did some hooting in appreciation of how much Jose hurt me.

Again I was left there just to be a point of entertainment to all the other guys and the girls. I just sat there suffering from that damn wood horse as well as all of the welts all over my back that are pounding and itching in pain. If the girls enjoyed watching me get punished they are having another great time today.

However, in spite of the girls being entertained, both Cally and I knew that my punishment was going to be extra severe that day as a result of me disappointing and disobeying Cally.

I was left sitting on that wood horse for what must have been another 5 minutes. The longer I had to sit on this piece of lumber the more it hurt. I can't even move even a little to adjust my position due to how tight my legs are being pulled by the straps that held me in place.

Rick picked yet another name from the hat, John, this time. I guess 35 licks was not enough as John went over to the hat and pulled out a number. John's number was 36, I started to cry again already just from the fear from getting 36 more from that damn whip, OH! OH! OH! it just hurt so much.

John came over and picked up the whip and looked at me and said that I haven't felt a thing yet, wait till I'm finished with you! I cried so hard you would have thought that I was actually being whipped at that minute and not just being threatened.

John, was about 6 foot 3 inches tall and weighed about 225 pounds and was all muscle and was right handed so he went around to my left rear side. WHACK! WHACK! WHACK! WHACK! WHACK! WHACK! WHACK! WHACK! WHACK! WHACK!

I could not tell if John was whipping me harder than the other two guys or if he was whipping over the welts that were already there. Either way, this session was hurting more the Jose's whipping did and that surprised me as I did not think that anything could hurt more than that.

WHACK! WHACK! WHACK! WHACK! WHACK!

WHACK! WHACK! WHACK! WHACK! WHACK! I was just slumped over again hanging from my wrist while moaning loudly after each loud and hard lick but had no strength to try and hold myself up, the only thing holding me up was the bondage straps holding my feet in place and the rope holding my arms up over my head.

I had not thought about the girls watching me get punished again and how humiliating that was and I was not thinking about anything except about how much that whip was hurting me. I was being punished so hard crying like a big sissy as I was just so beat up I wanted to pass out.

WHACK!!!!!!!!!!!! WHACK!!!!!!!!!!!!!! WHACK!!!!!!!!!! WHACK!!!! WHACK!!!!! WHACK!!!!!!!!!!!!! WHACK!!!!!!!!! WHACK!!!!!!!!! I had to accept John's 36 lashes to total 71 lashes altogether, how much more could I take?

Apparently a lot more, according to Rick as he pulled another name out of the hat and it was Oscar. Oscar pick 24 out of the hat and Rick told Oscar to use the strap instead of the whip. Oscar as also a big fellow, about 6 foot tall and well built.

Oscar went around behind me with the strap this time and WHACK!!!!!!!!!!!!!!! WHACK!!!!!!!!! WHACK!!!!!!!!!!!!!!! WHACK!!!!!!!!!!!!!! I could not control myself I screamed so loud I thought some neighbors a mile away may call the police. WHACK! WHACK! WHACK! WHACK! WHACK! WHACK! WHACK! WHACK!

Oscar finished with his 24 licks with that strap and I was just hysterical with crying and tears and screaming.

Does not anybody around here think that I have been punished enough? Sabrina and Ally sure did not think so as they got up again and gave Oscar a big round of applause.

Rick thanked all the guys for their participation and told them to go back to work. All the guys had to walk past me to get out of the barn and several called me sissy, faggot, etc. One guy said, WOW! you took a hell of a beating sissy.

About 10 minutes later after all the guys left and the girls were enjoying some ice tea, Rick said, alright then, my turn. I could not believe it as I was in so much pain from the whippings and the strapping and even that damn horse I was sitting upon.

Nevertheless, Sabrina and Ally both stood up and said that's right Rick it's your turn, you punish him good! I had no doubt that Rick would do just that as he thinks I hate niggers. I really don't have anything against black guys, I just have a bad habit of labeling people. I guess I watched too much "all in the family".

Rick picked up that big think strap and walked around behind me and OUCH!!!!!!!!!!!!!!!!! OUCH!!!!!!!!!!!!!!!! OUCH!!!!!!!!!!!!!! OUCH!!!!!!!! OUCH!!!!!!!!!!!!!! OUCH!!!!!!!!!!!!! OUCH!!!!!!!!!! I thought that nothing could hurt more than the last kid, but Rick, he was way better and getting that strap to SNAP!!!!!!!!!!!! SNAP!!!!!!!!!!SPAP!!!!!!!!!! across my back and I wished I would pass out but again I did not.

Rick punished me and punished me and punished me some more. If this did not make Sabrina and Ally happy nothing would I feared as I screamed until I was horse and I cried until I ran out of tears, but that did not seem to happen.

I had no strength to struggle anymore and just sat there on that horse with my legs holding me on that stupid wood horse with my hands being held high above my head with that rope.

I just cried and cried and cried and all I could here was SNAP!!!!!!!!! SNAP!!!!!!!!!!! SNAP!!!!!! SNAP!!!!!! SNAP!!!!!!!!!!!! SNAP!!!!!!!!!!! SNAP!!!!!! As that strap licked across my back.

After about 30 or 40 or maybe even 50 more licks I could see though my tears that Cally got up and she walked over behind me and looked at my back and told Rick that was enough.

To my surprise, all I heard from Rick was, yes Miss. Rick stopped immediately, I could not believe that Rick listened to Cally. Cally never seems to stop surprising me.

Ally then stood up and asked what happened, why did Rick stop? Cally told Ally that she told Rick to stop as he was going to damage me. Ally hollered back, damage the bastard, who cares, damage him good! Cally, in her firm tone, told Ally that was enough and to sit down. Ally immediately shut up and sat down. Again, Cally just keeps the surprises coming.

Rick released my wrist cuffs from the overhead rope and then hooked my hands behind me again. That put more pressure on my groin area from the wood bar as I could no longer lift any of my weight off the bar by pulling down on the rope, not even a little.

Rick led me back to the house and left me sitting out front on the wood horse as the girls met with and chatted with the Boss on the porch. About what I had no clue, but Cally did almost all the talking with the Boss. Anytime Ally tried to say anything, Cally told her to be quite an Ally obeyed Cally just like that.

Cally finally shook hands with the Boss and the girls said good bye to Boss and walked towards their car and Rick pulled me along with them so I could say goodbye at their car. As the girls were walking slowly to the car, a nice Lincoln Navigator that I paid for, Rick told me to thank them for visiting and tell them you hope to see them again real soon.

When we got to the car Sabrina came over to me and told me that her panties are soaking wet and she can't wait until my face is in her pussy for hours at a time. Sabrina walked away and I was left thinking why would I ever have my face in her pussy. There was nothing she could do or say that would make me want to lick her pussy for her.

I knew better that to try and do anything but exactly what Rick told me, so I choked out of my mouth, "thank you for visiting ladies and I hope to see you again real soon".

Ally looked at me and said that I was welcome and she will be happy to see me punished again in the future, you just wait till I get my turn she added! Again was I curious why she would ever get a turn?

Regardless, Ricks intention was to humiliate me one more time before the girls left and he sure did that pulling me around on that horse and making me thank the girls. But, DAMN!!!!!!!!!!!!!!! Sitting on this horse is getting more painful all the time!

Cally was the last one to stop by and she looked at my tear stained face and said, you know you brought this all upon yourself don't you? Yes, I whispered, from being exhausted from my beating but more so from all the shame I felt in front of Cally.

Cally, who brought her own car, told me that she was going to drive away with the others so that they would think she was leaving also, but that she would be back in 15 minutes or so, once she lost them in traffic.

Cally told Rick to take me back to the porch and let me off the horse and let me get dressed and have me wait for her in the corner. Yes Miss, was all Rick said. WOW! I thought, even Rick obeys every word that come out of Cally's mouth.

Rick got back on his horse and pulled me around to the front of the house and let me off the horse. I got dressed and went and stood in the corner and waited for Cally to return.

The only thing I thought of at that point in my life on that Reform Farm was that Cally seems to have taken over my life, just like she took over my life during the last year we lived together in my house. Cally seems to have everybody obeying her, even Rick and even the Boss.

Cally came back in about 10 minutes and told me to

come and sit next to her in one of the rockers on the porch. Cally, looked at me and told me that she now feels better about "US" and that she will be able to put my ABSOULTY STUPIDITY behind her now.

I smiled and told Cally that I was very thankful that she felt that way and that I would never do anything to give her "THAT FACE" again.

Sissy, I am glad to hear that, however, you will still need to sit on that horse for one hour per day, 30 minutes in the morning for breakfast and 30 minutes in the evening for dinner, for one week as additional punishment.

Cally looked at me waiting for me to complain or to see if I would beg her for less time, or no time at all. However, what Cally got was a yes Cally, and she could not have been more pleased as I saw that big smile of hers that I have not seen for about 6 weeks.

Sissy, Cally smiled at me and told me that she still really gets excited by my obedience to her. In Fact, sissy, if my pussy was not soaking wet from enjoying your punishment, it would be getting wet now.

Sissy, I would like nothing more right now then to have you lick my pussy for me and give me several orgasms. But, not today, I will wait until I get home and have Toni lick me instead.

I did not say anything, but I would have loved to lick Cally's pussy for her instead of Toni. Cally's pussy is the only pussy that I have ever had my face in and the only pussy I wanted to have my face in.

Alright, sissy, we have one thing to discuss before I leave and I want you to listen very carefully to me! Sissy, you have been here for only 6 months out of 48 months of you sentence so far.

During that time you have been nothing but disobedient and you have been severely punished for it. HOWEVER, SISSY, TODAY THAT ALL ENDS. Cally was taking that stern tone with me and apparently I like that tone from Cally as my cock started to get hard.

SO, SISSY, BEGINNING TODAY YOU WILL BE THE MOST OBEDIENT PERSON HERE! SISSY, NOT ONLY WILL YOU BE OBEDIENT, YOU WILL OBEY WITH A SMILE AND YOU WILL OBEY PROMPLTY AND YOU WILL EVEN ASK IF YOU CAN BE MORE HELPFUL!

Sissy, do you understand me? Yes Cally. SISSY, I AM NOT KIDDING, I WILL NOT CONTINUE TO COME BACK HERE AND VISIT YOU IF YOU HAVE ANY PUNISHMENT MARKS ON YOU! DO YOU UNDERSTAND ME, SISSY? Yes Cally.

Alright, sissy, I am going to leave now but I want you to get up every morning and say to yourself, what can you do today to be obedient and more helpful, EVERYDAY, NO EXCEPTIONS! EVERYDAY SISSY, HOW CAN I OBEY CALLY TODAY?

GOT IT SISSY? Yes Cally, I got it. Alright sissy, you can walk me to the car and maybe I will feel like letting you kiss me when we get there.

When Cally and I got to the car, Cally asked me what

was I going to do until the next time I saw her? I am going to completely obedient to you Cally. Alright, sissy, you may kiss me then.

I guess Cally really did forgive me as she let me lean her against the car and enjoyed kissing me for about 5 minutes until her tongue got tired and she told me that was enough that she needed to go left.

As I took my slow long high heeled walk back to the barn I could only think about one thing. OBEDIENCE, OBEDIENCE, OBEDIENCE! I had no intention of ever disobeying or disappointing Cally again, NEVER!

JANUARY 15:

For the last 12 days, I was the perfect obedient "girl" for Cally. Yes GIRL! I mean every morning after I would get dressed I would look in the mirror and see a girl. I looked like a girl, I walked like a girl, I waited on men all day in the barn like a girl in a restaurant. Even the guys treated me more like a girl, a girl named sissy.

I heard the name sissy so often and never heard the name Mort any more, even from Cally, that I started to think that sissy was a fine name for me.

I showed up to work early everyday and I was the last one to leave. I did not care what anybody had to say to me or how they said it. I gave them prompt polite service and then asked if I could get them anything else. I acted like I liked walking around in my girly clothes and truth be told, I really did.

The more time that went by the more I liked my girly clothes. Nevertheless, I always had this voice in my head telling me that I should feel bad and I should be ashamed of myself for liking me that way, as a real man would not enjoy himself being who I was being and looking the way I was looking.

At the same time, there was Cally's voice in my head telling me that she loves me this way and she wants me to be her girlfriend. At that point in time, I really had no choice in the matter. But, if it did, I think I would have been happier with Cally's voice then that other voice.

After all, when I do what Cally's voice says, I fell happy and content and satisfied with myself. When I listen to that other voice, I just feel bad, all the time.

Anyway, I was heading down to the house for my 2 pm visit with Cally and I could not have been more excited as I had not been punished for anything and I have been so extra obedient and I was looking forward to Cally knowing how happy I was to be able to give her such a good report.

In spite of my punishments in the middle of December and again on January 3rd, I really have not been disobedient since December 1st as the last two punishments were not about current behavior, but that December 1st problem. So, in reality, I have been good now for 6 weeks, the longest time so far since I have been here at the Reform Farm.

When Cally saw me coming she got up from her chair and met me at the top of the steps and gave me a big hug and kiss.

Sissy, do you have a report for me? Yes Cally I reported with a big smile. I have been completely obedient to you! That got me that big smile, that extra big happy smile that I always want to put of Cally face, the one that made me feel extra good.

That's good sissy, you have pleased me, so let's go inside and I will give you a surprise for you good behavior.

Cally and I went into the office and Cally closed and locked the door. Cally moved some things on the desk to one side and then laid herself across the desk on her tummy with her feet on the floor and with her ass bent over the end of the desk.

Alright, Mort, you may remove my panties and enjoy my ass. I was rock hard already and I got right down on my knees and I used my finger tips to slid Cally's panties down to her knees and flipped her short skirt up over her back.

I thought I was going to cum in my panties right there, right then, as I had my face right there at Cally's ass, the finest ass in all the land as far as I was concerned.

I kissed Cally's ass all over and thought it was the nicest thing that my lips had ever touched. I kissed Cally's ass with nice gentle kisses and then I gave Cally a few hickies and I even bit her a little.

Sissy, I did not bring any chocolate sauce with me, so I want you to use your cum to lubricate me. WOW! that was a new one. Nevertheless, I stood up and lowered my own panties and stroked my rock hard cock for less than a minute and then spurted all my cum all over Cally's nice round plump ass cheeks.

Get plenty in my hole, Cally told me. So, I got back down on my knees and use my finger to make sure I got plenty of my cum in and around Cally anus so the I could slid my tongue in and out with ease.

I was taking my time as I was planning to enjoy Cally's

wonderful ass for a long while. First, I took my good old time licking all my cum off of Cally's ass cheeks.

I loved being in that position, on my knees behind Cally's great looking sweet tasting ass and licking it and licking it and licking it some more. I had never tasted my cum all by itself this way before and I was not real fond of the taste.

However, that was not going to stop me from loving Cally's ass with my mouth. Even after I finished cleaning the cum off Cally's ass cheeks I still continued licking and sucking and biting them.

Cally was responding well to my mouth making love to her ass as she squirmed and moaned and wiggled her ass real nice for me. I finally stopped paying attention only to Cally's ass cheeks as I there were other wonderful parts of Cally's ass to enjoy.

I lifted my head up and took a couple of deep breaths and I just dove my face into the crack of two of the greatest looking plump but firm ass cheeks I had ever seen. I was getting my cum on my own cheeks, but I did not care, I just wanted to please Cally and by doing so I was pleasing myself.

I started to lick from the bottom to the top of Cally's fine ass crack. I licked along one side and then the other side and back again as I sucked up and cleaned off all of my cum.

After a few minutes, as the top of the crack was all cleaned, I started to work deeper. I used my tongue to lick deeper and deeper into Cally's crack until my tongue was all the way in and my face cheeks was firmly pressed against Cally's two soft ass cheeks.

I moved my face again from Cally's ass crack to take a breath or three. I used my hands to spread Cally's ass cheeks a little. Then I moved my face back into position and started to lick Cally's ass hole.

I licked up and down and all around Cally's ass hole and then I started to dart my tongue in and out of Cally's ass hole. I started to tongue fuck Cally's ass hole as well as I could and licked Cally's crack up and down and dove back in again.

Cally seemed to respond well to my efforts and was moaning and wiggling her ass real nice while saying OH! OH! OH!, YES sissy! YES sissy! YES sissy! Tongue fuck me sissy, that's it sissy, tongue fuck me!

Cally finally told me that it was enough and I pulled my tongue out of Cally's ass hole and lifted my face out of Cally's ass crack and took a couple of breaths and leaned back to wait and see how else I could pleasure Cally that afternoon.

Cally told me to get a warm towel and to clean her off. So I got up and went to the bathroom and get a nice hot towel and came back and got back down on my knees and took my time cleaning Cally's nice plump ass. I cleaned inside Cally's cleft and all around her anus as well.

Cally and I went back out on the porch and chatted about all sorts of things for over two hours. Cally showed me a few pictures of new house that I was still not sure why

I wanted, but Cally told me that I wanted it, so I guess I wanted it.

Maybe one day I will find out why I wanted a new house that I could not live in, but for now it was making Cally real extra happy and that was fine with me.

Cally said it was time for her to go and I thanked her for the special treat. Cally smiled and said that if I continue to be well behaved there will be more treats in the future. But, if I disobey her, even once, there will be hell to pay. YOU HEAR ME SISSY? Yes Cally.

Alright then sissy, So, what are you going to do for me until I see you again? Cally, I am going to be totally obedient to you! Good, sissy, that's what I expected to hear and that's what I expect to get, obedience and nothing but obedience so help you God.

I walked Cally to the car and we spent the next five minutes making out and then she was off and I was back to work in the barn.

CHESS GAME AND TWO CAININGS:

It was February 1st and I got though another two weeks with perfect behavior. I think that was the first time since I got to this Reform Farm that I did not have any punishment marks on my body.

I have been looking and walking like a girl for a couple of months now to the point where I started to think of myself as a sexy girl, as I thought that I looked like one in the mirror.

I wondered if that had something to do with my improved behavior as I did not seem to have any more trouble being obedient since I started to dress like this. I wondered if Cally had me dressed that way because she knew, or even thought, that it would help improve my behavior?

Anyway, the slow time in the barn was around 2 to 5 pm. Once I am finished cleaning up after lunch there is some flex time before I needed to set up for dinner.

In the afternoon the guys could stop by the barn and get some fruit and a drink, so they can be left out without me being there and I could clean up before dinner.

So, on a couple of occasions I had been called by the Boss to come down to the house and play chess with him. We would sit on the porch and enjoy an ice tea and a cookie or cup cake or two.

I did not need to try hard to beat the Boss, but I would keep the games close to keep him interested as I enjoyed playing. I also enjoyed speaking with the Boss as he was a pretty bright guy and we were able to talk about a lot of different things. There was no one else I could really have a intelligent conversation with, except for the days Cally visited.

This one day while we were playing chess, this young boy showed up. The Boss greeted him in a very friendly way. It turned out that it was Rick's brother, Robert, The Boss introduced Robert to me as the Boss said, you remember the story I told you about Rick's brother?

The Boss asked Robert how he was feeling and Robert told the Boss that he was almost all healed. Miss Anne got him a drink and he sat down to watch us play chess.

About 10 minutes later I could hear a horse coming, which turned out to be two horses with Rick and Pete pulling each of the white guys behind their respective horses.

Pete got off his horse and had Jerry take off all his clothes and then strung Jerry up to the roof rafter that extended over the yard. While Rick made Greg strip down and bound him over the hitching post.

Rick got the big long think cane and started to cane Greg about as hard and viscous as you could imagine.

Rick gave Greg one THWACK!!!!!! about every 6 seconds or so or about 10 THWACKS!!!!! per minute.

Robert watched with pleasure as Rick just kept up a steady THWACK!!!! THWACK!!!!! THWACK!!!!!! THWACK!!!!!! THWACK!!!!! with about 100 THWACKS. Rick only stopped once to change sides, so beat Greg for a solid 10 to 12 minutes.

When Rick finally stopped, the welts on Greg's ass were so big and bright and very angry looking. About 100 angry painful welts. Greg grunted and yelled and screamed a lot throughout the entire caning, but he did not cry, not a tear.

Nevertheless, I enjoyed watching Greg get that caning and I did get an erection and maintained it the whole time. I wondered what that may have meant? But, there was no answers for me and I guess it did not matter all that much.

Pete let Jerry down and brought him over to the hitching post. Rick unhooked Greg and took him back over to the rafter and strung him up with his caned ass facing us.

Rick bound Jerry to the hitching post and then gave Jerry the same hard caning that Greg just got. Jerry grunted a whole lot and yelled some but did not scream and certainly did not cry at all.

When Rick was finished beating Jerry, his ass looked as bad as Greg's. Both of their asses were nothing but welts on top of welts from side to side and top to bottom. I would guess that it would take more than two full weeks for all those welts to fade completely.

Robert seemed to have a real nice time watching those two white guys get that beating as part of their punishment for beating him up for no reason in the first place.

The Boss told Robert that he could come back in three months and Rick would beat them again for you. Robert smiled and thanked the Boss and went and spoke with Rick for a few minutes and then left.

The Boss and I played chess for another hour. Rick and Jerry took the two white guys away, but I saw them both standing in the corner each evening during dinner for the next five nights.

FEBRUARY 8th, CALLY VISITS:

There was not much to report to Cally for the last 3 weeks. I got up every morning and worked all day every day well into the evening in my girly clothes and my five inch high heels. I seemed to like these clothes and my heels more all the time.

I was so good and so obedient that I even worked on my day off. I figured that everybody had to eat anyway and I had nothing else worthwhile to do, so I may as well work and make sure I did not get into any trouble.

The Boss called me down to the house a couple of times to play chess. He never wins, but I guess he thinks he is getting better so he keeps trying. I tease him now and then and tell him that even a little girl like Cally could beat him. He takes it well.

So, that day I made plans for the Boss to play Cally. Cally did not know that I strung the Boss along to keep him interested and Cally beat him three straight games in under an hour.

I watched the whole thing and laughed my ass off quietly the whole time as Cally just pummeled the Boss with no mercy. I was so proud of her.

Cally showed me some pictures of the house progress and it was starting to look real nice as the outside was finished already, complete with the roof. Now, they just needed to work on the inside.

After that fun was over, the Boss left us alone and Cally asked me about my behavior which I was proud to say had been perfect.

Cally was happy with my report and took my inside to the office and gave me a nice blow job as a reward.

We went over some bills that Cally paid, nothing unusual, Cally certainly was no spendthrift.

Cally showed me my Brokerage statement and again there was too much money in there. With that Big smile that I love so much on Cally face, she told me that she bought a gold option and it paid off 9 to 1, so she put up $10,000.00 and got back $90,000.00.

Another $90,000.00 Cally made for me. That bring the total of extra money the Cally made for me in under 8 months to $445,000.00.

Again, I asked Cally if she wanted any of the money and again Cally told me that she had everything she needed and wanted, except me being home with her.

Cally and I spoke for another two hours out on the patio and then Cally needed to go and it was time for me to set up for dinner.

FEBRUARY 21ST,

I had more perfect behavior to report to Cally this time and I knew she would be please and so was I. It seemed that being obedient, although very hard sometimes, was still much better than getting punished. Once again, I wondered if it had something to do with me dressing and looking like a lady?

I always thought that Sabrina and Ally were pretty stupid to get punished so often as I always thought that all they had to do was obey me and they could avoid all that pain and humiliation.

I guess I found out that it is not all that natural to be so completely obedient to someone and I have figured that out the hard way as well. So, maybe they were not so dumb after all. Or, was I just as dumb?

Every time I see Cally I think that she is prettier than the time before, today was no exception. As I walked down the driveway and saw Cally just sitting there in a rocking chair I got an erection.

Neither Cally nor I had anything to really discuss that day. I told Cally about my behavior and she was so pleased. I asked Cally about how everyone was doing in college and she told me that after that spanking that she gave Ally back in November, that Ally was getting mostly B's and a C in math.

However, Toni, who was feeling fine was getting all B's and Mindy and herself get mostly A's and a B here and there.

Cally, and you? Straight A's again! That got a big smile from both of us as we were both real proud of Cally.

We sat outside and enjoyed the weather, had a ice tea and some chocolate cake and chatted about many other things for a couple of hours and it was time for me to get back to the barn for dinner service.

Cally took me inside first and gave me another one of her great blow jobs for being such a "GOOD GIRL" as she said.

As I walked Cally to the car she did ask about how I was feeling being dressed as a girl all the time. I blushed bright red and had to admit to Cally that I actually liked it.

Cally gave me a big smile and told that was great, that she was hoping I would feel that way.

Now, sissy, what are you going to do until I see you again? I will be totally obedient to you, Cally. Sissy, and who will be totally obedient until I see them next time? Again, I blushed brightly as I felt the humiliation in my face. Your "GOOD GIRL" Cally.

Very good, sissy, that's what I wanted to hear.

As I was walking back towards the barn I was thinking that Cally always calls me sissy, as if it was my name and not a description. I wondered if that would continue in the future. Not that I had a problem with it, I was sort of use to it by now. Just like I was use to wearing all these girly clothes.

MARCH 5TH, CALLY VISITS:

There was not much going on over the past couple of months worth nothing as everybody seemed to be behaving. There were very few punishments and there were none for me as I have been the perfectly obedient "GIRLFRIEND" to Cally.

I walked down from the barn at my usual time about 2 pm to meet Cally. Cally jumped up when she saw me coming and gave me a big hug and a real nice kiss.

Cally then took a step back and, sissy, how you been my GOOD GIRL? I smiled as Cally called me sissy again, but I responded, yes Cally. Oh, sissy, you don't know how that pleases me and excited me, more than you may ever know, sissy.

We sat down on the porch and chit chatted a little while about a few things, mostly about how excited Cally was about the new house and it's progress.

We went over some bills and my brokerage statement. I asked Cally if she had any additional information concerning the Boss's lawsuit? Cally said she was told that the Ex federal judge that she hired for an opinion gave the opinion to the Boss's attorney. However, she was not told what the opinion was or if it would help.

I asked Cally how she was making out with Sabrina. Cally told me that Sabrina is alright. Cally said that she could always get a better maid, however, Sabrina knows everyone and get along well with everyone and does an adequate job.

So, sissy, until my sissy maid is ready to take care of me, I will just keep Sabrina. I just looked at Cally as there she goes again talking about having a sissy maid and I was pretty sure she meant me. But, that was not going to happen so I said nothing and enjoyed looking a Cally looking at me seeing if I was going to respond.

We went inside and Cally gave me a choice. I could either have another blow job or I could masturbate on her ass again and lick her to my heart's content.

I was surprise by my answer, as even without thinking about it, I chose to enjoy Cally's ass. I found that surprising as I was actually choosing to do something for Cally instead of doing nothing and getting a great blow job for myself.

Cally looked at me and said that is an interesting choice, sissy, very meaningful. Maybe to Cally I thought, but what did it mean? I had a great time and I must have spent a good 15 minutes with my face on or in Cally's great ass before Cally told me that was enough.

When we got to Cally's car, Cally told me, sissy, it has been since December 1st that you have been disobedient. Your continued obedience to me I find very complimentary and very exciting and you know what I mean by exciting.

So, sissy, if you can remain obedient for one more visit, I will let you lick my pussy next time I visit. Cally was making me so happy and I thought that was strange as eating pussy was never anything I really cared to do, but with Cally, I felt like it was a real treat.

MARCH 25TH, CALLY VISITS:

Today was Cally's last visit before my April 1st punishment for the girls pleasure. On the bright side it has been 3 months on a row now that I have not been punished for anything and both Cally and I were very happy about that part.

Once again I questioned myself if it had anything to do with me dressing, wearing a wig and makeup, and looking like a girl that has allowed me to be so obedient? Or, was it my increased desire to obey Cally and be her "good girl"? Maybe both.

Either way, we were both happy with the result. I have been dressing and wearing my wigs and putting on makeup now for five months as well and over all I was extremely ashamed to admit that I liked looking like a girl and dressing like a girl.

I was finding that I liked the way the guys treated me better and the way they looked at me, as well, with lust in their eyes. But, overall, I liked my high heels and my skirts and I liked my big chest and my trim tummy being on display with my midriff tops.

I felt much more sexy and I liked it, sorry for Mort, and, good for sissy, I guess. Mort almost seems like a different person from my past.

Well, I guess Mort was a different person from my past.

After all, Mort was that Bad Boy who took advantage of Sabrina and Ally and who was getting punished himself all the time after he was arrested and sent here to the Reform Farm.

While, sissy, she is a submissive and obedient "Good Girl" that makes everyone happy including herself. But, most important, sissy makes Cally happy!!!!!!!

I met Cally at our usual time and we enjoyed a nice kiss and hug on the porch and then sat down and chatted for a while. Cally found out that I have been her perfect obedient "girlfriend" and she was so pleased.

Sissy, you do remember what I told you last time you could do if you were obedient again when I got here this time? Cally, how could I forget, that's all I have been thinking about for the last 10 days or so. And, Cally, what an extra motivation you gave me to be obedient.

Alright, sissy, I really do not have any news for you about anything, so let's go inside and you can have your reward. Cally, me, and my rock hard erection went inside and Cally took me right to the guest bedroom like she owned the place, strange, but then with Cally I always seem to find the unexpected.

Cally pointed to the side of the bed and told me to wait there. As I waited, Cally slowly took off all her clothes and just teased me with her body. Cally's find breasts, Cally's great thighs, Cally's ever so delicious pussy. I was again surprised that I was not coming in my panties, I was so excited.

Cally laid down on the bed and just pointed to her pussy.

I climbed up on the bed, between those soft luscious thighs of hers and put my hands up under Cally's nice plump ass cheeks and started to sniff Cally's fine and already juicy pussy.

I started to just use my lips by kissing gently on the inside of Cally's right thigh and then slowly used my tongue to lick up and down on the inside of Cally's very nice left thigh to just below Cally's beautiful pussy lips, Cally moaned just a bit.

I did the same on Cally's right thigh again and Cally wiggled just a bit more. Then I started to kiss Cally again but more strongly all along the inside of Cally's thighs alternating between the right thigh and the left thigh, the left thigh and the right thigh.

Slowly I moved my mouth up towards Cally's pussy and started to kiss first her pussy lips and then licked the outside of Cally's pussy lips, first the right side and then the left side, kissing and licking and kissing and gently licking and kissing some more while I used my hands to start squeezing Cally's ass cheeks ever so gently.

I moved to the front and inside of Cally's pussy lips and began kissing and licking and licking and kissing both the front and the inside of each pussy lip. While at the same time, I would use my hands to adjust the pressure against my mouth by squeezing tighter or relaxing my hands against Cally's ever so fine ass cheeks.

Cally was squirming and moaning a little more. I started to lick Cally's pussy lips a little stronger now and licked from the bottom to the top like a lolly pop and pulled Cally tighter to my tongue with my hands and that got more of a reaction out of Cally as Cally started to squirm more, moan more and even moved my hips involuntary.

I kept this up for a minute or so and I kept going deeper and deeper with my tongue with each lick until I could not get my tongue inside of Cally's pussy any deeper. I pulled Cally even closer with my hands thereby pushing my entire face into Cally's pussy. I licked Cally a bit more while moving my head back and forth back and forth like a tiger tearing apart a piece of meat.

I started to lick around Cally's clit but did not touch it yet. I thought that I was exciting Cally and at the same time frustrating her and that was my goal, just as I saw Toni do.

All of a sudden, I guess Cally could not take any more of my teasing of her pussy and started saying NOW sissy! NOW sissy!

I immediately started licking my tongue all over Cally's clit and Cally exploded all over my face in wave after wave after wave of orgasmic delight.

I laid my head down on the inside of Cally's thigh and just stayed there with Cally until she was ready to move again. Cally sighed and breathed heavy and then said, Oh sissy! Oh sissy! That was great!

Cally tapped me on the top of my head when the time came about 3 or 4 minutes later. I moved back into position and licked Cally very aggressively this time to see if she like it and Cally responded very well to me obvious desire to please her and was coming again all over my mouth in less than three minutes.

Over the next half hour I put my mouth and tongue to work pleasing Cally's pussy for her five times until Cally seemed exhausted and told me to clean her.

I went and got a hot towel from the bathroom and very gently cleaned Cally's pussy of all her joy juice and then dried her off and helped her off the bed so she could get dressed.

We got some ice tea and some chocolate cake and settled in on the porch and enjoyed the weather and chatted about many things. My cock was still rock hard and even though I surly did enjoy pleasing Cally with my lips and tongue, it was not helping pleasing me cock.

Cally did not seemed inclined to give me a blow job like she usually does and I knew that as long as I was in prison, Cally was not going to let me fuck her. So my cock was just left rock hard and ready for something that was not happening.

As we chatted for a while my cock finally gave up and shrunk down leaving a nice sticky pre cum puddle in my panties.

When it was time for Cally to leave, as I walked her to the car and we hand hands my cock came alive again anticipating kissing Cally.

When we got to the car Cally took her hand and felt my rock hard cock. Cally asked me if I was expecting some pleasure for "HER", meaning my cock. I did not want to seem like I was complaining, so I just shook my head yes.

Cally smiled and told me that I need to learn how to please others without expecting any relief for myself. Then I will be able to love her better.

I was not sure what Cally was talking about, but then a lot of what Cally says makes no sense to me until later when I figure it out.

Alright, sissy, we do need to discuss you 9 month punishment next week. Sissy, I know it will be very painful and this time it will be extra humiliating for you.

However, sissy, I do expect you to accept it as well deserved punishment for your past mistakes and I expect you to be completely obedient. Understand sissy? Yes Cally.

This brings this book,

The Bad Boy Gets Punished, Two

    A sissy maid missy bad boy series, part five

To an end.

The next book,

The Bad Boy, The sissy Maid,

A sissy maid missy bad boy series, part six

will pick up with sissy (Mort) getting punished for his 9 month anniversary at the Reform Farm. Very punishing and very humiliating. You will not want to miss that and many other upcoming surprises.

Also included;

The Boss has great news and then has secretes with Cally,

Sissy maid missy's training begins,

Sissy maid missy's maid service begins,

Maid missy and the laundry,

Cally meets sissy maid missy for the first time,

Maid missy struggles with her sex lessons and gets punished,

Maid missy needs to practice and practice some more to give better blow jobs,

Maid missy gets a new dress and is taken out in public, But gets the cane first as missy struggles with her obedience.

Maid missy learns to please Miss T's ass,

Maid missy learns to please Miss Anne's pussy,

Maid missy needs more blow job practice,

Cally visits maid missy again,

Maid missy goes to the Laundromat, this does not turn out well for her.

SPANKING DIARY

A sissy maid missy series, part one

SPANKINGS AND SUBMISSION, TO MY WIFE

A sissy amid missy series, part two

A SISSY MAIDS LIFE

A sissy maid missy series, part three

A SISSY MAIDS LIFE, TWO

A sissy maid missy series, part four

A SISSY MAIDS LIFE, THREE

A sissy maid missy series, part five

The Bad Boy and his French Maids

A sissy maid missy bad boy series, part one

The Bad Boy and his French Maids, Two

A sissy maid missy bad boy series, part two

The Bad Boy and his French Maids, Three

A sissy maid missy bad boy series, part three

The Bad Boy Gets Punished

A sissy maid missy bad boy series, part four

The Bad Boy Gets Punished, Two

A sissy maid missy bad boy series, part five

The Bad Boy, The Sissy Maid

A sissy maid missy bad boy series, part six

The Bad Boy, the sissy Maid, Two

A sissy maid missy bad boy series, part seven

The Bad Boy, the Sissy Maid, Three

A sissy maid missy bad boy series, part eight

The Bad Boy, The Sissy Maid, Four

A sissy maid missy bad boy series, part nine

The Bad Boy, The Sissy Maid, Five

A sissy maid missy bad boy series, part Ten

A sissy maid missy bad boy series, continues.